And Then You Apply Ice

Stories

Pamela Gwyn Kripke

OPEN
BOOKS

Published by Open Books

Published by Open Books

And Then You Apply Ice is a work of fiction. Names, characters, places and incidents are the products of the author's imagination or are used fictionally. Any resemblance to actual events, locales or persons is entirely coincidental.

Interior Design by Siva Ram Maganti

Cover image © by Ittikorn_Ch
shutterstock.com/g/Fon+Nongkran+PMM

For my daughters, Daphne and Cooper,
whose strength and spirit inspire me no end

Several of the stories in this book were previously published. "The Suitor" appeared in *Book of Matches*, Issue 5, Spring 2022; "Promenade," in *The Barcelona Review*, Issue 101, 2021; "And Then You Apply Ice" appeared under a different title in *Folio*, Spring 2020; "Beauty Queen," in *The MacGuffin*, Vol. 38, No. 3; "Matchbox," in *Brilliant Flash Fiction*, January 2022; "Behind the Wheel," in *The Concrete Desert Review*, Issue 2, Fall 2021; "Shadeland," in *Round Table Literary Journal*, Volume 56, Spring 2022.

CONTENTS

THE SUITOR

My mother had boyfriends, some of whom she had to my childhood house for meals. Her dating felt weird, but I tried to act as if it didn't. So, when she asked if my husband and I would come over and have dinner with Jerry Shaps, I imagined nothing more agonizing and tragic but agreed to attend anyway and decided to make a pie. Then, I asked her about Jerry Shaps, feigning average interest.

"He looks a little like Cousin Betty," my mother said.

"Cousin Betty is a woman," I reminded her.

"Yes, and he looks like Cousin Betty. Without the pearls."

"She's kind of pretty."

"Gorgeous," my mother said. "Just gorgeous."

It wasn't as if she forgot that she was married for forty years, to a man she met as a teenager. Mom just wasn't the mourning type.

My husband and I arrived ahead of Jerry Shaps that night, to help set out hors d'oeuvres and crack the ice. When my father died, he didn't know that I disliked my husband, to whom I had been married for three years. I didn't tell him because he was sick. Being sick was bad enough. My mother's Jerry Shaps dinner occurred eight months later, too soon for me. But I knew that the timing of the dinner was not up to me. My mother's mini skirt was not up to me. My father's early death was not up to me. What was, I knew, though I preferred to ignore it, was my own ridiculous marital state, a condition characterized by resentment, ill will and scoffing. So much scoffing.

Mom made the orange chicken, and the house had the dinner

party smell. Salmon mousse to start, spinach souffle on the side. Apple crisp at the end. The apple crisp was insane. I wore white pants and a white sleeveless top.

"You look like a cigarette," Hal, my husband, said.

My mother took a necklace off her closet doorknob and lassoed my head. Then she swiped my cheeks and nose with a huge brush.

"What are you doing?" I asked.

"Close your eyes. It's shimmer." The brush could have painted a residential hotel. "Now you're a person."

The doorbell rang. Jerry Shaps.

My mother descended the stairs, and we followed behind. She pushed up her hair in the mirror by the last step. My face itched.

Jerry Shaps smelled like the musk that teenagers wear.

"This is my daughter, Whitney, and her husband, Hal," my mother said, taking Jerry Shaps by the elbow. Do not touch Jerry Shaps, I thought.

He held out his hand, my mother still affixed to its adjacent forearm.

"I love your name," he said to me.

"Thanks. It's for the museum."

I lifted my hand to meet his.

"Museum?" he said.

His lack of cultural awareness became, in that instant, the least affecting of his attributes, as the spore-producing organisms inhabiting his nail beds lunged at me in full force. Microbes and microbes of fungal material had set up shop in the tips of his digits, the very digits on their way to meet mine. They came at me like poisoned arrows, encrusted yellow and diseased.

"The Whitney," I said, stopping the forward motion of my arm.

He remained confused. "Not the singer?"

Hal stood next to me and caught sight of the fungus on Jerry Shaps, the fungus that *was* Jerry Shaps, as far as I was concerned. The thing that worked about my marriage to Hal was that we both noticed the fungus at the same moment. This sounds like a highly specific situation, observing the contagion on the fingers of one of my mother's widowhood boyfriends, but Hal and I had mutual radar for disgusting things in general. We smelled decaying chipmunks in the yard, sweat on household repairmen, rancid dairy products...at the exact moment in time. We saw splats of excrement on the street, tripe in a butcher's case, untreated elephantiasis...precisely at once. Our sensory receptacles were harmonious. We perceived repulsive stimuli in tandem and with identical effect. I had hoped that this common awareness would extend beyond the grisly, maybe to matters of loyalty or generosity or love, even.

"Oh, a museum makes sense," said Jerry Shaps. "Your mother is artistic."

My hand was now eleven-point-eight inches away from Jerry Shaps. Bacteria crumbled from cracks in the nails, forming sandy piles, like rat droppings. Across the cuticles, vertical cuts split the skin, a railroad track of infection. Jerry Shaps' arm hovered at ninety degrees from the torso, parallel to the foyer's quarry tile and in the ready position. I needed an out. A sudden cough and its subsequent mouth-covering would appear contrived, but no other excuses presented themselves quickly enough. I inhaled and constricted my throat, pushing my tongue back into my oral cavity to give the sound more heft and urgency. Perhaps heft and urgency would be convincing. Perhaps Jerry Shaps would recoil from the sound, himself, thinking that it was I who was repulsive and avoiding my hand before I avoided his.

Having seen the fungus when I did, Hal had an identical window for conceiving a plan, but I saw no movement in my peripheral vision. No shifting of weight, no flapping of limbs. I heard no distracting chatter, no exclamations—"Look! An otter in the living room!"—no grunts from phony indigestion. In previous such situations, Hal had risen up and intervened, despite the tension elsewhere in our relationship. He had snatched me by thigh and waist and flown me over oozy pools of sewage. At cocktail parties, he had whacked kabobs of uncooked poultry to the floor, excusing his clumsiness with charm and paper towels. This time, for the first time, I was in it alone. Hal would leave me exposed, choosing not to help me, deciding that I should fend for myself or maybe, not caring if I did or didn't. For spite? For self-importance?

I stopped myself mid-breath, deciding not to let out a hefty and urgent cough in the foyer of my childhood home. Lungs inflated, chest plate lifting, I saw Whitney Houston in my head. On a stage, under the lights. Whitney Houston would rise up tall, throw her shoulders back. Steal the room, do the thing, some way, the possible way. Artifice had no place here, she'd tell me—*no place here, baby, no place*—kicking out a strappy heel, flicking a wrist.

I pulled my hand back from Jerry Shaps' reach and angled it firmly into my pants pocket. Saying nothing, I planted my feet in front of the closet, inside of which I knew my father's wool coat still hung, his umbrella still leaned. A surgeon, Dad had pristine fingers and nails and palms, scrubbed and sterilized, soft, exacting, virtuous. His driving gloves, into which he secured these magnificent instruments, sat high on the shelf, one atop the other, digits lined up. Sentries, they perched behind me, palms pressed like prayer, hidden. My mother, distracted by her hostess duties, didn't notice when Jerry Shaps collapsed his arm or when Hal dropped open his jaw and muttered something about politeness and being ridiculous and *Jesus, Whitney*.

I remained in front of the closet as Jerry Shaps ushered them all away into the living room. Both hands in my pockets, elbows wide, I stood watching them go, pretending that Jerry Shaps was some other kind of man in my childhood home, that he had been lost and rang the bell, and we let him inside because we trusted him. I pretended that the correct man was just late coming in from work, delayed at the office or deep inside someone's abdomen or in traffic on the parkway where it creeps at that curve with the pine trees. With the pine trees and the pretty brook that lights up orange if you are lucky enough to see.

PROMENADE

The milk runs out at night. This is the worst time.

No, late afternoon is the worst time. You have the option, then, to go outside and walk to the store, so you dwell on the decision, choosing not to go and feeling more annoyed about it in the morning than you would have had the milk run out at night. The milk presents a personal dilemma, one that can affect your sense of productivity and purpose. It can make you think about other choices, all of your choices, ever, since birth. It can make you think about your capacity to act in a beneficial way.

In Manhattan, dogs cannot enter stores with milk in them, even small stores, neighborhood stores, bodegas. The signs are clear. No dogs. We love your dogs. But no dogs. So, if you fail to get the milk in the late afternoon, you will have to make two trips in the morning. You will have to walk your dog in the manner to which he's accustomed, return him to the apartment and leave once again, retracing your steps to the store. You will do this all without coffee or tea, because you didn't have the milk.

On one such day, Caleb woke up and took Marvin on his preferred route past the mayor's house and down the hill to the promenade, where he enjoyed watching the tugs churn up the East River. Marvin, a strangely hirsute labrador of questionable origin, stopped to view a barge slide by, earlier in the day than one would typically sail. Marvin liked boats, and there was no hurrying him, not that Caleb would, even on a day requiring the two outings. Caleb indulged Marvin's predilections, believing that human companions had a duty to respond to their dogs' requests so as not to frustrate them. All creatures need to be understood, Caleb believed. The barge was huge, blocks long. Marvin watched its entire passage, sitting down at one point, unaware that Caleb had the second trip for milk yet to make. Caleb hadn't mentioned it.

When Marvin could no longer see the barge, he stood up from the pavement and resumed his walk.

"That was a long one," Caleb said to him.

Marvin glanced at Caleb, equally impressed.

They passed the grassy patch where the woman did Chinese dance routines to music from a cassette player. She had excellent technique, and Caleb thought that she must have been in a troupe when she was younger. He imagined her moves done in unison, multiplied by hundreds, ribbons, scarves, parasols flying about.

A bit farther down, they passed the curvy steps. Some dogs enjoyed climbing the retaining wall, making many S shapes. Marvin never attempted. Not one for ramps.

The morning traipse was a trance for Caleb and Marvin. Their six feet fell into a cadence. Their chests floated identically through space, still and solid. Their thoughts meandered and grew, transcending the daily concerns, becoming more profound in the air than they were at home.

Marvin chose the route past the apartment buildings beyond the southern end of the park, which would keep them along the river. When it was gustier, he turned west for the trees, seeking protection. People installed mirrors on their terraces, so they could see the water even from their sofas. Some decorated their railings with shells and starfish, even though it was a river they lived on and not a sea. One porch had an imitation anchor hanging on the brick wall. Okay, that could make sense.

Just as Caleb and Marvin passed the imitation anchor, a shoe slapped onto the pavement in front of them. Marvin startled and looked to the sky. Caleb checked left, then right. Seeing no one, let alone someone with only one shoe, he turned and looked behind them. No foot in sight. It was a woman's shoe of average size, a loafer, thin-soled. Tan, with a gold chain. Marvin sniffed the instep and returned his gaze toward the building, several stories up. He tapped his front feet on the stone beside the shoe and barked. Clipped, stern barks. Warnings. He paced, forward and back, now whining. He picked up the shoe in his mouth and threw his head back, like a horse, unsettled.

"What, Marvin?" asked Caleb.

Sirens.

Caleb crouched, following Marvin's line of sight, shielding his eyes from the sun smacking the windows.

Marvin placed the shoe down and barked again. Quick, high-pitched barks. Affirmation.

Louder sirens, slamming of doors.

Marvin grabbed the shoe, bucked his front legs, eyes trained on a terrace three floors up. A foot stuck through the railing. A foot with no shoe. A mirror revealed its calf, a knee, a skirt.

People gathered on the promenade. A policeman appeared at the terrace door. Marvin clenched the loafer, breathing heavily, whimpering. Caleb bent and held him, stroked his head. The chain on the shoe trembled. They would have to return it, somehow. The woman would want it back. It was a new shoe. Maybe she tripped or fainted, watering plants before work.

"She'll be okay, Marvin."

Emergency medical people appeared in the mirror and squatted down, forming dark humps in the glass.

"The dog has the shoe," said a person by the river, pointing.

Caleb heard and turned his head toward the man.

A second policeman appeared in the terrace doorway. The emergency people stood and sank again. The exposed foot did not move.

Caleb's knees hurt, and he stretched to a stand. "Let's go home now," he said to Marvin.

Marvin extended his front legs, pressing his belly onto the pavement.

"The dog has the shoe," the person by the river said again.

Marvin looked up at the foot.

The entrance to the building was around the corner off the promenade, and Caleb and Marvin had gone by it many times, typically during their evening stroll. Just a few buildings flanked the walkway, and the one in question was the newest, squeezed in between two elegant pre-wars some time in the seventies.

"Let's go, Marvin. Got things today."

Caleb had lived in New York for twenty years and had seen plenty of police tape. Though curious about what happened in his neighborhood, he was not an ogler. Marvin, though...he was some ogler. A professional. "Let's give that back," Caleb told him. "You've seen enough."

Marvin's body remained taut. Saliva dripped down the instep of the shoe.

"He's not budging," said the man by the river, his leg tucked up under him on the wall.

Caleb, sufficiently diverted from the morning routine, did not respond. Participants, now, he bemoaned. Ten years earlier, when he was forty-five, Caleb's wife left him for a high school classmate, deciding after a weekend reunion to move to Western Massachusetts and live on his hydroponic farm. She couldn't make a salad with bagged lettuce, but she went to live on a hydroponic farm. Their one child, now twenty-eight, adopted Marvin for her father, concerned that he had become isolated. Treacherously isolated, in a way that could make him sad and tip him over. An accountant, Caleb worked from the apartment, communicating, commiserating, commingling with numerals, to the exclusion of most human beings. He did well with people; he just didn't choose to interact with them on a regular basis, and his daughter interpreted this preference as an emotional liability. Marvin, as she had hoped, drew her father out of the house, though he could not persuade Caleb to engage with anyone, and truly, he did not want to. Engaging was to be done with Marvin.

The man by the railing was right. Marvin was not budging. His eyes fixed on the terrace, where the authorities made their way inside, leaving the woman prone on the floor.

"I saw it," the man said to someone else. "Like a rag doll. Horrifying."

Caleb overheard and waited.

"Who knows, jumped, probably. Or pushed, though I doubt it."

What the man said confused Caleb.

"From the top floor," he heard the man say, turning to see him pointing to the roof of the building. Caleb counted the stories. Nine. He took Marvin's face in his hands and stared at him. Saw his skin pleat above his eyes.

"Jesus," he said, realizing that the woman had fallen and become tangled up in the terrace on her way down. He shuddered and sat on the pavement next to Marvin, grabbing him around his chest.

Marvin pressed his torso into Caleb's thigh and released his grip on the shoe, placing it on the cement in between his legs. He kept his gaze on the woman. They sat for two hours, one lump of a body, in the middle of the promenade. They sat until the policemen took the woman inside, at which time Marvin rose up. Caleb followed, patting down his pants, taking his hat off and putting it on again. Marvin picked up the shoe and began walking, back the way they came.

"Maybe leave it now?" said Caleb, not sure.

Marvin held the shoe and continued to walk, eyes trained. He led Caleb to the corner and turned a sharp left toward the building's entrance, the gold chain lit up in the sun like a flare.

DRESS FOR SUCCESS

The guests begin to arrive at the Victorian mansion that we rented for the wedding. I hear their heels on the hardwoods from a room off the foyer, where a staircase clings to the walls and climbs high, its white balusters prim and obedient. When my mother isn't looking, I whisk under the steps and into the ladies' lounge, fully dressed and crowned, a tulle rosette the size of a water taxi stuck to the top of my head. I pull seven hundred layers of organza up from the floor and back my rear end onto a sofa in the center of the room. The fabric shoots up around me like a Venus Flytrap.

My concern at the moment is keeping the yardage as far as possible from my lips, which had been painted in a fifties-style pink, a hot cerise. Fearing blotches on the hem that was now encircling my cranium, I stick out my chin, suck in my cheeks, and fend off the barrage of silk with my forearms, attempting to remain calm, and more important, sane.

After a few minutes, or years, the door opens. A little girl walks inside, stops just past the threshold and stares. What are you doing, she seems to ask. And do you know that you are doing it? Do you think that you should be doing it? Now? Here? Tangled up in a taffeta haze? I hadn't seen her before. I hadn't invited a little girl to the wedding. She doesn't smile, or ask to touch the dress, or clasp her hands in front of her chest, the way little girls do when they see a princess. She doesn't say anything, and I don't either. We just look at each other, and then she turns on one foot and leaves.

How I get from the sofa to the back of the aisle in the mansion's library is unclear. The trip from back to front is even grainier. While walking toward my groom, I feel a throbbing in my neck so robust that I think an artery will burst, spewing shoots of blood onto the diagonal lines of pearls that wrap my torso. The pounding crescendoes as I reach the end of the aisle, where I envision myself lying on the floor in a fluff of organza, now crimson, with six hundred cocktail napkins pressed to the hole in my neck. My father lifts the veil to kiss my cheek and I wonder if he, a thoracic surgeon, can sense the arterial unrest beneath my skin.

I won't die in the rented mansion on the Hudson River, I assure myself in front of the altar, but will be treated on the very sofa in the ladies' room, revived by the eighty-nine physicians in the family who had ripped tourniquets from the hems of the brides-maid gowns. My dress, though, will remain a casualty, drenched and limp from the geyser spraying from under my chin.

I remain upright during the ceremony and hear nothing of what anyone says, my mind settling instead on which hospital will be chosen for me, the closer one in Tarrytown or the major medical center a greater distance away in Valhalla. I feel certain that my dad et al will stabilize me well enough to make the longer trip to the teaching facility, academia so revered in our family, particularly during crises. Mom will carry the suitcase full of bathing suits and mini-skirts that we had packed for the Caribbean. I will be released a few days later in a wheelchair, sporting a violet bikini with triangle clasps.

"Whitney, do you realize that you just got married?" my high school friend Richard asks on the receiving line.

I grab his hand. "Feel my neck, right here. Do you feel it?"

"Feel what?"

"The pulsing."

"I don't feel pulsing."

"C'mon, Richie, you graduated from med school." I move his fingers toward my ear and push them into the glands that swell when you get sick. "It's like a bass drum. Boom. Boom. It feels like it's going to explode."

"Whit, get a grip. There's nothing wrong with your neck." Richard hugs me, losing his face in the wads of fabric surrounding my head. "Just shake some hands. Eric," he calls over his shoulder, "let's find the shrimp. Whit says there's lots of shrimp."

––––––––

The kind of bride who does things that other brides do not do, I eat everything in sight—the grilled steak and the crispy potato mélange and every last string bean. I consume the salmon cake, with greens, ahead of the entrée and devour a double-size chunk of the iconic cake afterwards. Also, I do not hold hands with my former boyfriend/now husband, or kiss him, except at the altar when there is just no way around it.

The pounding in my neck subsides as the evening wears on. We dance, and people make toasts about the hard work that marriage is, and I throw the bouquet and everyone leaves. Mom and I go into the bathroom, where I had stashed a bag of clothes. She helps me take off the dress, and I put on a pair of drawstring pants and a sweatshirt. It feels as if I had performed in a dance recital, fancy hair and makeup still intact. We sit on the sofa, and she puts her arm around me.

"I saw a little girl in here before."

"Really? Maybe she came with one of the staff. Little girls love weddings."

"It was strange; she looked spooked. Did you see her anywhere?"

My mother shook her head. Then, she said that she and Dad would be leaving.

"Where? What do you mean?"

"Home, sweetie. Time to go."

"Now?"

I walk my parents to the front door of the mansion.

"Love you, baby girl," Dad says.

They kiss me and head out to their car, centerpieces and paper bags of leftovers cradled in their arms.

––––––––

My new husband and I arrive at the hotel room, and I change into a college tee rather than the lingerie I had received at the bridal shower weeks before. I lie in bed next to my mate, the boy I have chosen to be with forever. All brides must feel numb and muddled with the transition; it will be better when I adjust to the notion. He is a good person, yes he is. He has been a terrific boyfriend, someone who has doted on me, fed me, hung pictures on my walls. I have enjoyed the condition of girlfriendness, loved the balloons sent to me at work and better still, the scene on the bus when I tried to get them up the steps. He will be as competent a spouse as anyone, even though it took me three days to say yes. Even though I have absolutely no urge to touch him. I will want to touch him tomorrow, probably.

I roll over and see the dress draped on a chair. I close my eyes and see it whisking to the ladies' lounge, the scalloped hem quivering behind me. I see the sofa, feel my lips purse. And I see the little girl's face, her blunt bangs, her sullen gaze. I don't know if a little girl walked into the ladies' room in the Victorian mansion where I was married. Or if the little girl was me.

Saturday Night Live intro music plays on TV. Bruce Willis is hosting. I love Bruce Willis.

AND THEN YOU APPLY ICE

In bed, he fluttered her fat between his thumb and third finger. Jane was thin, 105-pound thin, but he found the places where the flab collected. Everybody has the places, he told her another time when they were not in bed, even people you might think are anorexic. Really, anorexic? He fluttered her fat after they had sex, typically. He fluttered it fast, bee-like. She had the deposits at the top of her thigh, in the back, toward the inside. He knew the exact location, and he could probably gauge the amount. The grams. Or when it was liquified and sucked out, the milliliters. Fat is measured as volume, not weight, clinically speaking.

Stan gave his patients bottles of their fluid fat to hold for a photo, following its removal from their bodies. He showed the pictures to Jane on a Sunday afternoon when it was raining and they were sitting on his couch. One woman gripped two bottles from their necks, clear plastic like for fancy water and nearly full. The liquified fat is yellow, tinged with pink, from the blood. The woman smiled a drugged-up smile, standing in a hospital gown with the blue diamonds on it. Stan had a place in the fat-sucking room where he stood up the people when they could get off the table and not faint from the mild sedative. The mild sedative that did not make them fall asleep while he inserted the lasers, but let them talk about how they would wear the skinny jeans or how they hated to exercise so they never did or why their husbands annoyed them. "So it won't come back?" they asked Stan while mildly sedated, "even if I eat doughnuts?"

Stan had the patients hold their fat as proof that he had taken it out of their abdomens and thighs and buttocks. People liked to complain that Stan hadn't done what he promised to do. He hadn't filled up the lines around their eyes with enough chemical gel or burned off sufficient layers of skin from their jowls or reduced the flapping under their chins to just a wobble, a wobble that they could deal with, if they had to, if the totality of the flapping couldn't be obliterated as they had originally hoped. Stan was not a magician, he liked to say. But he thought the people looked better when they left, so much better, exponentially better. Jane couldn't always discern which was the Before photo and which was the After.

"This one?" she'd ask. "No, wait, this one?"

Her inability to instantly and accurately see how much the faces and bodies of Stan's patients had been improved irked Stan. No, infuriated Stan. Made his voice go up in pitch, made his pigeoned-feet strut around with speed, made his comments sharp and his own fat quiver around his mouth.

"You're saying I'm bad at what I do," he'd say. "You don't know anything about what I do."

"No, she just looks pretty good in both," Jane would say.

When Stan first fluttered Jane's fat at the back of her leg, they had been dating for about a year. She rolled to her side and lifted her knees up to make it hard for him to continue. She thought it was an odd way to be touched, but she didn't say anything. It was late, and she had a lot to do the next day, and Stan was a good guy, in the ways that mattered to Jane.

"Good night, Jane Jenkins."

"Good night, Stanley Ross."

The fifth time he fluttered her fat, she sat up and turned on the light.

"Why do you touch my leg that way?"

"What way?"

"You fiddle with the fat. Do you do that to your patients?"

"Of course not, that's crazy."

The following weekend, Jane and Stan met for dinner. Jane felt like dressing up a bit, wearing a ribbed black top and platform boots. She spent extra time on her makeup, experimenting with a chisel-point eyeliner and mascara that she had read about in *Vogue*. A painter, she knew color and form and proportion and light, and she was adept with a brush. Used one always for her lips, that night a teaky red. The mascara required two steps; the results would be dimensional. Sumptuous. Mega-sumptuous.

She whisked into the restaurant, a tony storefront Italian. Her cape flew in behind her, charcoal, edged in black velvet. Nice contrast for the lips. Not a dramatic personality, Jane liked looking that way. People noticed. She knew it, but she wasn't a snoot. People had noticed since she was a child. It was just how it went. Jane, the pretty girl. The Pretty Girl.

"I can't sit near the kitchen," said Stan when he saw her enter. "It was so noisy last time."

"Okay, sure," said Jane. "And hello, Stan."

He took off his coat. "Do you want to check that?"

Jane unwrapped herself and gave Stan the cape. She bent to gather it up so it wouldn't drag on the floor.

The hostess led them through the center of the narrow restaurant to a table toward the back. Jane felt festive in her platform boots and ribbed black top and chisel-point eyeliner, walking that way, the party way. They sat and ordered a glass of wine.

Jane had spent much of the day sending photographs of her paintings to galleries, hoping to spark interest. She had gotten some positive feedback, but nothing more. One day, her work would hang and people would come, she believed, or had to believe, and they'd tilt their heads and nod, talking about the color and form and proportion and light, pointing, turning their palms up and back. For income, she taught art at a high school, a job that, combined with her frugality, had supported her and her two children for sixteen years, even sent them to college. Stan offered a lifestyle that she couldn't afford herself. He had asked her to move in with him, but she said that she wasn't ready, that she needed her own place to paint, her own furniture, her own quiet, all of which Stan said he'd provide.

Jane had said that she loved Stan, even though she didn't want to grab his shirt and kiss him. She thought that maybe she didn't love Stan after all, but she also thought that she simply preferred living without a man in her house, whether she loved him or not. She was confused, and because she was confused, she did nothing.

Stan jerked his head around and shot a look at the chair behind him.

"Can you move back a little?" he asked Jane, pushing the table toward her. Quickly, Jane grabbed her drink.

"Forget it, let's switch," he said. "Can't deal with getting slammed." He popped up and found the hostess at the front of the restaurant, leaving Jane at the table and knocking into the man behind him. Stan waved to her to come. Hurry, he mouthed. Jane apologized to the man.

"I want to see you suck out the fat," Jane told Stan when they sat down again.

"Really?"

"Something about it," she said. "It's so primitive."

"What do you mean? I have to be highly trained, you know."

"I'm not saying that *you're* primitive," said Jane. "But the concept is so...I don't know...crude. Primal."

"That makes no sense. It's a technical medical procedure."

"It's not the procedure. It's the notion of it," said Jane. "But forget it."

"I have to be accredited, you know."

"I know. You're not understanding what I mean."

"So, you don't want to come?"

"No, I do."

That week, Stan checked with a patient, Eileen, to see if she'd allow Jane to watch when Stan melted the fat out of her lower abdomen. Eileen said that she didn't mind. Two weeks later, Jane arrived at Stan's office and changed into the scrubs that were waiting for her at the reception desk. Eileen had been prepped, drawn upon with a black magic marker, given the mild sedative. Jane waited for the nurse to retrieve her from the consultation room, where she sat on the chair the patients sat on, imagining what they might say to Stan — Dr. Stanley M. Ross — upon first meeting him.

Maybe: "I hate my knees. And I hate my eye lids, and I hate how I look in everything. I can't get dressed."

Or: "My husband cheated on me with our son's violin teacher and now I can't stop eating. Look at me, I'm disgusting."

Or: "You have nice skin, Dr. Ross, but I'm sensing that you

could be short-tempered and judgmental."

Wait a minute. They wouldn't say that. Would they say that? The door opened.

"Jane, come with me," said the nurse. "He's ready."

Eileen's lower abdomen was centered on the operating table. She wore bikini underwear, socks and the robe with the blue diamonds, rolled up to her breasts. The rest of her body was exposed. Jane had painted many models, in a variety of positions. She had painted many "reclining nudes," like Eileen. "Reclining Nude With Limited Will Power." People look better when they are lying down. Gravity pulls their fat into the surface beneath them and stretches out any lines or bulges in their skin. When they stand, gravity doesn't work in the same way. It doesn't eliminate the lines and bulges for some reason. Gravity is gravity, and it shouldn't matter which way a body is positioned, so this is perplexing. It's also why women who think they're fat lie down a lot on the beach. They don't play Frisbee.

Jane stood quietly against a countertop, near the door.

"I'm going to be making a small incision now," Stan told Eileen, pressing the tip of his scalpel into her flesh. "And another."

Eileen's lower abdomen didn't look so flabby to Jane, though she saw it only in the recumbent position. It appeared that a few solid weeks of jogging, maybe two miles a day, would do the trick. And the carb thing, of course.

Stan reeled out yards of clear tubing from a machine, the end of which was outfitted with the laser. He looked happy, holding the rod parallel to the floor and inserting it into Eileen. One of his hands pushed down on her belly, and the other maneuvered the wand, sliding it forward and back, like a cellist. Suddenly, the tubing stiffened and gurgled. Sputters of the liquified lipids made their way first, followed by full blasts, at times pure yellow, at times stunningly pink.

Jane had seen the photos, so she was prepared, as prepared as an abstract painter mom could be, but the gush of red into the tube unsettled her. She had left her sweater on underneath the scrubs, thinking that an O-R could be chilly. She pushed up the sleeves and pulled at the neck. Stan continued to rake Eileen's insides with gusto, forward and back, unaffected by the blood spurting into the bottle on the floor of his operating room. The nurse, Dawn, sopped up the incision site with gauze. Eileen winced, and Stan told her that everything was going well, that she was looking beautiful. She was looking beautiful now. He glanced down at the bottle to see how much fat he had collected. Jane felt sweaty, on her forehead, under her arms, between her toes. With one hand, she held onto the counter behind her and forced herself to breathe in deep. Chills. Sweat. Chills. Next would be the fainting part, so she bent forward and dangled her head upside down, pretending to fix something on the hem of her pants.

"Just a few areas left," Stan said, pulling the laser out of the hole in Eileen.

Jane rose up to see him pause and flutter Eileen's fat between his thumb and third finger. He fluttered it fast, bee-like, determining where to direct the heat. Where to correct the imperfection. Where to eradicate the flaw. Dizzy, Jane slid her back on the counter toward the door, felt the knob in her hand and slipped out.

In the bathroom, she stripped off the scrubs, her sweater, her bra. Naked in front of the mirror, she cupped cold water from the sink onto her face, her neck, her lower abdomen, her thighs, the tiny rivers hugging the contours of her body as they dripped to the floor.

THE HILL

To say that Whitey was just a dog, a gigantic or colossal dog, even, would be like saying that a chimpanzee is just a smart monkey, or a thoroughbred a sporty horse. It would be the same as saying that Renoir's work was colorful. Debussy's, creative. It would understate his essence, his force, his power atop the mountain on Bayberry Way and in life. Whitey was iconic. He was fear and doom and domination, spiraled up together like tornado currents in a field. This is what I thought of when we traipsed over petunia beds and jumped through the sprinkler, whether Whitey was circling in his cage or not. This is what I thought of when we burned leaves and sledded on the side of the house, and when I went to sleep in my bed, wrapped in pink gingham like an egg roll from Tung Sing. I thought of Whitey, getting out.

The people who owned him lived in a red brick house, the back of which we could see from below. On certain days, the man led Whitey to the cage on a leash, secured him inside, and walked back across the lawn to his door. The days and times were unpredictable. I could not determine a schedule, though I was kind of young to decipher behavioral patterns in adults who incarcerated their family pets. I would have done better at nine, maybe. What I did do was tell my brother to sweep the area before venturing out.

"Matthew, go check."

"He's not out there."

"Look again. Please."

I waited by the sliding glass doors in the den as my brother went in and out to investigate and report back. He humored me, not as petrified of Whitey as I was. I was truly comfortable only when Whitey was not in the cage, when he occupied space elsewhere in the universe, say, on a train bound for Canada or at a kennel for mammoth dogs who scared little girls. I didn't even like it when he was simply inside his own home. He could careen through the bay window or crawl up through the chimney and stand on the roof. Whitey had that ability, that supernatural other-worldly capacity to transcend the natural course of things. He was not a dog, or a wolf, even, but some other being who had lost his flock and parachuted into suburban New York without warning. Needless to say, I stayed away from the hill when Whitey was in the enclosure. Somehow, though, I mustered the bravery to play on our lawn below. Trapped, we both were, in our own worlds.

One day when Whitey was out, Matthew and our next-door neighbor Brian broad-jumped from one level of the hill to the next while I played on the swings, as far from the pen as possible. I enjoyed the typical tricks that kids learn and perfect on the school playground — the backward lean, the spiral, the flying dismount. At home, I developed another move, achieved with not a small share of practice. After reaching the height of the arc, I shifted the weight of my body enough to twist the seat and cross the chains, once, turning me backwards for the reverse trip. The challenge was to exert just enough energy to rotate only one time, such that the trajectory of the swing remained consistent and I could unravel with similar ease on the other side. After much repeti-tion, and more than a couple of collisions with the equipment's iron frame, I could perform the trick handily. In backward flight, however, I could not see Whitey's cage.

I pumped my legs hard, swinging high in the corner of our yard. Matthew and Brian jumped from the fourth tier to the third, then the second, and skipped over the first to the lawn, where they fell and rolled and tackled each other. Brian had more muscles than my brother had at seven, and he clicked his cheek several times a minute, turning his mouth into a sideways apostrophe. He showed up at our house often, and unexpectedly, slipping in without announcement and staying, sometimes, until it was dark.

The man came out with Whitey as my swing chains untwisted and I swiveled around. I felt the shudder in my breast bone, the

punch of nausea I'd later experience at the prom or in Greg San-
born's dorm room. My legs tucked under the seat; I flew back.
They straightened out; I soared straight up, eyes on the figures
moving at the crest of the hill. They were deliberate and solid, like
soldiers in a processional. The leash was short, wrapped around
the man's left hand. Whitey took long strides, never veering, never
changing his pace. He held his head up, shaking it once or twice
and returning to position. Proud and firm, an innocent prisoner.
His color was striking for a shepherd, chaste and saint-like, yet
aberrant, wild.

"Whitey's out," I called to Matthew.

He and Brian stood up from the grass, looked toward the
cage and continued their wrestling. My legs slowed, and the
pendulum shrunk.

"He's out."

Matthew and Brian rolled around and grunted, swatting and
grabbing each other's bodies.

"Stop making so much noise," I yelled from the swings.

The man didn't turn to look at us down the hill. He didn't show
any discernible emotion on his face. He approached the cage as
he typically did, reaching his arm out straight to grab the gate.
He clawed the chain link at chest height and drew it toward him,
stepping back. The sides of the enclosure were tall, fortunately,
and I appreciated the consideration given to the design, at least.
When the gate opened, Whitey stepped across the threshold into
the pen while the man stayed put at the opening, the leash unwind-
ing in his hand until it was slack. Whitey stood, waiting for it to
be released from his collar. Then, immediately, he began to pace.
The man pushed the gate shut, latching it with a shrill. He walked
back toward his house just as he had come, disappearing from
view behind a sawed-off hedge. Meanwhile, Whitey ringed the
perimeter of his cage, gathering speed, like a show pony under a
tent. I slid off the seat.

Matthew and Brian had stopped tackling one another and
were throwing a ball; one stood on the hill, one on the lawn. I
walked toward the patio, not sure what I'd do when I got there.
Hopscotch, maybe. I kept a box of chalk on the patio, near the
steps to the kitchen door.

The streak of white, when it appeared in front of the cage, on the safe side, our side, lodged itself in my belly and my brain. I stood, stiff, as Whitey oozed down the incline, low and slinky, rattling my understanding of the universe, my universe, to its core. He did not bolt, but escaped stealthily, as if he knew he had crossed some line. Some either-or, right-wrong, good-evil. What should be-what shouldn't. I screamed to my brother, chills spilling through my limbs, sweat washing me cold. Whitey lifted his jaw and extended his legs, becoming taller, faster, finding a stride in the uncharted terrain, in transgression. I took off across the lawn, watching his descent to my left, seeing boys jump and scatter, a baseball roll. You don't run from an animal, we had been told, except when your body commands that you do, that you run like you have never run on any yard or any playground or end up eaten or dead or changed some way forever. You run when you are eight and even when you are not. You run. Away.

Matthew, Brian and I blasted toward the patio. Whitey was just feet behind my brother, keeping an even pace, growing in size. I hadn't been so close to him, hadn't smelled him, seen the saliva drip off his tongue, the muscles flex. The sliding door could have been on another continent, and my feet felt glued to the flagstone, the way legs don't flutter when you are drowning in a dream or arms don't wave when you need them to fly. Brian barreled toward the door, thrashing his arms. Without slowing, he smashed into me, knocking me to the stone and lunging for the handle. Matthew, steps behind, pulled me up and pushed me across the threshold. We burst into the den and turned, throwing our bodies onto the glass and shoving it shut. Scrunched together at the seam, where door meets house, we stood, heaving, eye to eye with Whitey from behind the divide.

I felt the blood drip down my leg. My palms burned. My body shook.

"That was close," Brian said.

Matthew narrowed his eyes, out of breath. "You didn't have to push her."

"I didn't push her."

I ran upstairs. The window in my parents' room looked out onto the backyard. I stood and waited to see if Brian would leave or if Whitey would climb back up the hill or if the man would discover him missing and wade down through the bushes to get him.

I told myself that he was simply looking for companionship, wanting to join a pack since he spent so much time alone. I told myself he was exploring down the hill the way we explored up and maybe, having watched over us, he felt that we were, in fact, his responsibility rather than his prey. I was certain that he would have attacked us on the patio behind our house on Bayberry Way, but I told myself he would have stopped in time or sniffed us and turned away or grabbed a stick to play with instead.

I pressed my face to the window and peered down. Whitey was nowhere I could see. Brian was nowhere I could see. Look both ways before crossing, stand back from the stove, I had been told. The peril wouldn't intrude, despite the monster circling above. How dare Whitey steal that security. How dare he show me that my fear was warranted. Everyone said it wasn't. Everyone said it was fine.

THE SWATCH IS NOT NEARLY THE WHOLE THING

Julia climbed the three flights to her apartment, key in hand. She did not notice that the door across from hers was cracked open and that an eyeball peered out. She did not know that the eyeball watched her leave in the mornings and return in the evenings, her forearms lined with the tell-tale emblem of her trade: the showroom shopping bag.

Afflicted at the age of six, Julia attached to fabric swatches, paint finishes and graph paper like a moth to a cozy iridescent. By twenty-four, she had lived a life among the bolts of damask, chintz, brocade, the laces and eyelets, the broadcloths and shirtings and wools. The yardage that underpins 39th Street, and 38th, and parts of 40th, down into the earth and up where it's sticky and silent, where the rolls lean like tipsy soldiers, cardboard hats poking from their uniforms, sequinned dates unraveling on their arms.

Despite a college degree in aeronautical engineering, Julia's enchantment with interior spaces and their contents propelled her to the holy altar of design, the D&D building at 59th and Third, where she secured an impossibly precious internship with one Mavis B. Sloane, the late-eighties Doyenne of Decor. The Arbiter of Arrangement. The Savant of Style. What Mavis B. Sloane bestowed in cachet, however, she did not pay in pesos, necessitating the walk-up apartment with the ever-widening fissure on the ceiling over the tub, not to mention the eyeball behind the door across the hall.

Julia rented Apartment 4C on the day that Mavis B. Sloane hired her, and with help from her friend Henry, she left the studio she shared with two tap dancers on the rise and moved in the following week. Without her knowing, the eyeball observed the carrying of cartons, the wheeling of suitcases, the sliding of mattresses. It saw eagerness and ambition, the churning of ideas, all raised to skin level, pink and dewy in their emergence.

"Henry, the nesting tables," Julia called down the staircase, leaning over the railing. "The chinoiserie!"

She met him halfway and together, they carried the three pieces, bubble-wrapped into a cube. Hints of red lacquer floated under the plastic, snapper in a sea.

"Finally, these are going in *front* of the sofa," said Julia, beaming. "Lined up in all their glory."

"A statement," said Henry. "So you!"

They reached the landing. The eyeball looked at Henry.

Julia brought the tables inside. There was no true foyer (she would have to create one with some relic, a sidelight maybe, or a tablecloth of her grandmother's), so one entered into the kitchen, which led to the living room, which led to the bedroom. A railroad flat, Julia's first on-her-own New York City apartment had turn-of-the-century charm, though not much light, as is standard for a linear space with just one street view. An additional casement window overlooked the air shaft in the living room, providing a sooty breeze and not much else. Julia carried an umbrella every day that she went out, unable to see the sky to determine whether it was needed. On the sidewalk, in the glaring sun, she stuffed it into a shopping bag rather than hike it back up the forty-eight steps.

Julia and Henry finished carrying her belongings up from the vestibule, unaware that they had been watched the entire time. Henry helped position the couch and bed and then left. In the hall, he heard a latch and turned toward the eyeball's door. The white parts of the orb lit up in the beam from the fixture overhead. Taller than the eyeball, Henry lowered his line of sight and inched toward the glinting ivory triangles. The eyeball did not flinch. It did not close the door and lean up against its back, caught and mortified. It held its gaze. Brazen. Henry returned the stare and swiveled away smoothly, his tennis sneaks tapping as he descended, the interior door slamming shut at the bottom. He would not tell Julia about confronting the eyeball, as it may have made her nervous. In college five years earlier, a boy trapped her in his off-campus apartment, a room in a house on the east side of Providence. He pushed her down, held her down, pressed himself, rubbed himself, helped himself. She got away from him and ran out, past the smirks from other boys in the front room, pulling on clothes, covering her face. She hadn't lived alone since.

Inside the apartment, Julia dusted the moldings and sills, swept and mopped. She scrubbed the fridge, stove, shower and sinks. Wiped down the closet, lined the shelves. The eyeball had retreated and reappeared several times while she worked. By evening, Julia had unpacked every garment, stacked every plate, hung every painting, having determined where each would go on hand-drawn lay-outs devised during the week prior. Surroundings should feel unceremonious, according to Julia's design philosophy, yet they should be planned. Julia had no patience for so-called artists who entered a room and felt things...the tug of a slipper chair there, a double-tiered table there. Objects, and their dimensions, imposed decisions based upon balance, mathematics, quantity, shape, and these decisions required preparation. This is not to say that Julia wasn't spontaneous or, God forbid, "uncreative." Her brand of artisticness was rooted in order, its security spurring her to be clever and innovative, despite what more whimsical colleagues may have thought.

She fell asleep that night under a pale paisley cotton duvet, filled with an all-season down alternative chosen for its economy and fluff. Each day, she hurried out her door at the end of the hall with one goal in mind—arriving at the showroom ahead of Mavis B. Sloane. One morning, after two weeks in her new apartment, Julia dropped her umbrella while locking up. Rising from the terrazzo, she saw the white triangles flash from its strip of air. They widened and held still. Julia stopped, curved in a crouch. She reached behind her and jiggled the knob, checking that it was secure. The eyeball did not blink. Julia scampered down the steps. Outside, sun swatted her in the face, and she jammed the umbrella into a swatch-stuffed bag.

At lunchtime, she walked eleven blocks south and met Henry, who had walked eleven blocks north.

"My neighbor stared at me today," Julia said. "Through a crack in the door."

"Did he say anything?"

"Nothing, not a word...if it's a he. But it was really kind of disturbing."

"Sounds disturbing, but I wouldn't worry about it. Probably just your average New Yorker."

Julia ascended the stairs in the evening, key in hand. She could see from the top step that the eyeball was not out. Quickly, she made it into her apartment, but before locking her door, she inched it open again, her own eyeball pressed into the sliver of air. The neighbor's door was now ajar. Still wearing her jacket and holding her bags, Julia scanned the strip, top to bottom, halting at a shine just a few inches above the knob. Lower than the morning. Squatting? Kneeling? Weary after a day? Shrunken after a day? Creepier after a day?

Julia pulled away and slammed the door, hoping to seem formidable.

Later, under the pale paisley cotton duvet, she named the eyeball Iris.

"Screw you, Iris."

In the morning, Julia looked through the peephole before doing anything else, before peeing or brushing her teeth, before turning on the news, making tea, taking a shower under the fissure in the ceiling. Deciding to keep a running list of Iris sightings, she placed a pad of paper on a slim shelf in the entry, which she had marked off, ultimately, with a swag of crepe de chine. Having never seen the rest of Iris, Julia did not know if she was in fact a female eyeball, but she chose, consciously or not, to believe that she was.

After six days of data, a pattern emerged. When Julia left, Iris materialized twenty-four seconds after the turn of the knob. Upon her return, Iris appeared at the moment Julia's foot reached the forty-seventh step.

"Good evening, Iris," Julia said on the seventh day.

The oval turned round.

"Good morning, Iris," she said on the eighth.

The oval narrowed to a squint.

After work, Julia bought a medium-sized television and took it home in a cab. She would position it on the etagere, second tier from the top, across the room from the sofa and red nesting tables. At each landing, she set down the box to refresh her grip. At the top, she slid it on the tile to the end of the hall.

The lid lowered. Lashes.

"It's a TV, Iris," said Julia from her coir Welcome mat. "*You* should know a TV when you see one, of all body..."

Blink.

"Look at you. That's a first."

Iris cocked.

"Good night, Iris."

Julia went to Hastings-on-Hudson that Saturday to visit her parents. She stayed overnight in her childhood room, a vestige of her floral fixation, if not a psychotic interpretation of the traditional design scheme. It looked as if the Tuileries themselves had burst from a cannon.

"Take this beautiful English ivy to the city," her mother said.

"But there's so little light."

"You'll find some," said her mom, wrapping it up in plastic. "And you will love it. Every house needs a plant. Needs life!"

Julia took the ivy, knowing that it would not provide life, but death, certain dried-out death in her dark walk-up, requiring an extra hike to the trash outside. On the train, she decided to relocate a tiny tray table to a spot in front of the bedroom window, where the plant would have its best shot, if temporarily. Oh, to flourish in the time that you are given.

When she reached the forty-seventh step, she did not see Iris, but a slim streak of yellow light outlined her own door. She slowed her gait, shifting the plant to free up her hand. The door was clearly open. She stopped. Gasped. Felt her skin contract, shiver. Not knowing whether to enter, she placed a palm flat on the wood and lined up her eye in the crack, seeing the ledge in the entry, the stove, her cookbooks. Someone had unlocked her apartment, been in her apartment, maybe, probably. She swiveled her head. No Iris.

"Did you see?" Julia yelled, her body tense.

Nothing.

"Iris!"

The apartment ended behind the door. Julia flung it open and pressed it against the wall, squeezing the intruder, if one was hiding. She propped the door with the ivy pot, slung the shower curtain, grabbed a rolling pin from a drawer, hollered random threats and made guttural lunatic sounds as she was taught to do when she moved to New York. She hurried through the kitchen and into the living room, where electrical cords hung down the front of the etagere, books lay cockeyed on the shelves, vase shards peppered the floor. She snatched the phone from its cradle and ran back into the hall to call the police.

The invasion pierced the sanctum that Julia had created, wrecking her order, her geometry, her inspiration. Worse, it imposed the fear that the burglars wanted her, and not her belongings. The girl's not here, so let's take her TV. Isn't that what violators really want—the body? The flesh and the psyche, a double win. You can worry about electronics or jewelry for only so long, but skin, bones, tendons, nerves, those are forever.

Julia heard steps on the staircase and startled. Two police officers appeared at the top. Iris' door clicked open.

"You must have seen…" Julia said but caught herself, thinking how it might look.

The officers walked past her and went inside. They determined that the thieves likely entered through the air shaft window, from the roof, and exited through the front door.

"Did they want me?" Julia asked. "Did they want to hurt me?"

"They wanted your stuff, and now they have it. They won't be back."

"Are you sure?"

They nodded.

"Someone could have seen them," said Julia.

The policemen looked up from their notes.

"Across the hall. A person, no, an eyeball watches me. All the time. When I go in and out. Maybe you can ask."

One looked at the other. "Okay, sure, we can ask."

"Yeah, sure," said the other.

Iris was out when the policemen left. Through the crack in her door, Julia watched the men pass right by her and go down the steps, not asking, not looking.

"Wait," Julia started to say but didn't, the molding tapping her lips. She glared at Iris, and Iris glared back.

BEAUTY QUEEN

It was not enough to play some chords on the guitar and sit down, or do a couple of cartwheels, like the other eight-year-olds. For the talent component of the Miss Towanda Beauty Pageant, I played a Beethoven Sonatine on the piano and a Haydn fugue on the clarinet. To solidify the win, I also sang, performing the school-age favorite, "I Know an Old Lady who Swallowed a Fly." For the piece, in which the Lady ingests eight animals—fatally—I wore a poster board, upon which a gargantuan stomach had been drawn and punctured with small holes. With each line of lyrics, I hooked on a corresponding sketch to the belly that consumed all but my head, forearms and feet. I know an Old Lady who swallowed a spider; I attached a spider. Swallowed a bird; bird. Ultimately, the animals all hung from my torso. I didn't act out the dead part.

For half the summer, my father was the doctor at Camp Towanda in Honesdale, Pennsylvania, where kids slept in bunks and played newcomb and wore work boots in the rain. My mother went along for the month, and with little to do in the infirmary, she hatched schemes such as the above. For the bathing suit portion of the beauty pageant, she sewed balloons—immense inflated balloons—onto my red swimsuit, front and back. It was inconceivable that I would lose. It was inconceivable that I would emerge of right mind. I felt bad for the other girls who probably should have won, being normal and on their own.

When my name was called, the camp director put a crown on my head, cut from green construction paper and painted gold.

She handed me a bouquet of wild Pennsylvania weeds and turned me by my shoulders to face the crowd, squeezing my bones with her fingers, pulsing with excitement. I held the weeds straight out in front of me, resting my forearms on a balloon sprouting from my ribs.

"Go ahead, Lizzie" she said into my ear, "take your walk."

The weird guy who was in charge of canoeing turned on the sound system and blasted the pageant song. "There she is..." the audience sang, yelling over the "America" part. I stood on the stage, unable to move my feet. "There she is....Miss TO—WAN—DA—AAAHHH."

"Go, go," the director said again, pushing on my spine.

A raised runway had been built in the center aisle of the rec hall. Boys sat on the left, girls on the right, like the religious sects. I looked for my parents, but the spotlights made it difficult to see. The losing contestants filled the stage behind me, crowding around in their unadulterated bathing suits, looking pretty happy and carefree despite their defeat. I was a shoo-in, and they knew it. I had whipped them with a display of nepotism, not to mention aid and assistance, that Camp Towanda hadn't before seen. I stood motionless, feeling the floor rumble with their jumping and danc-ing, with their holding of hands and swinging of arms, with the frivolity and camaraderie that did not include me. Me, the victor, the model of camper girl perfection, the paragon of beauty and skill. They were over it. They were done considering me, in any way. In all ways.

I attempted an escape into the wings, but the camp director lunged and caught my arm. Remaining on the stage, ignored by the loser contestants, was a sub-optimal option. I slipped free of her grip and walked toward the runway, assessing its height off the floor. I was confident that I could leap the three feet but would wait until I was parallel with the side door, which was left open for ventilation. My first thought was to seek refuge in the girls' bathroom across the lawn, but I sensed that such a place would be where the people would naturally look. It's where the people would think to converge in a hunt for an eight-year-old Miss Towanda Beauty Queen pocked with inflated balloons.

I stepped onto the runway. The younger kids sat in the front rows. I peered down and saw the girls from my bunk, the ones who nominated me for the contest. Thank you very much, girls from my bunk. Each age group put forth its own representative, so I had beaten not only other elementary schoolers and pre-pubescents but a thirteen-year-old, too. A veritable adolescent with training bras and underarm growth that I stared at when we changed in the lake house for swimming. A girl who actually wanted to talk to boys and had earrings and the pads from the drugstore that my mother kept under the sink and didn't tell me about, despite my inquiries, my thousands of inquiries. I had beaten a fellow camper who wore lip gloss. Lip gloss!

The rec hall's side exit was in view, but not yet within leaping range. As always, it was propped open, manned by a counselor on each side. I would fit through the doorway, I assured myself atop the runway, even in my distended state. When I got to the row where the ten-year-old boys were sitting, the cheering welled. As I approached them, The Middies, the ones on the end bolted up from their benches. They hollered and lurched toward me, tripping over each other to reach into the aisle, yelling at me and swatting. The Middies tried to pop my balloons.

When my parents' explanations about the female reproductive organs left me more confused than I was previously, I asked Mrs. Perryman the next time I went to her house to pet her spaniel, James. My parents let me cross the street and walk four houses down, ring the bell and ask to play with the dog, which I did several times a week. Mrs. Perryman was nice about it every time, pulling the door open in her cigarette pants and looking surprised even though she probably wasn't. When I asked her why the older girls could skip swimming, she startled a bit but said that my mother should tell me. Then she hugged me, which she had never done before, and said I could take James out on the leash, which I had never done before.

Several of the Middies' hands reached me and smacked the balloons. I felt the tug on my swimsuit. I felt the fabric drag down over my skin and pull away from my body, letting the air in, making a gap, uncovering me. I felt the elastic on the leg opening ride up and twist, but I couldn't reach far enough over the balloons to readjust it. The boys' counselors grabbed them back by their shirts, and they fought it, stretching out the fabric like sails in taut wind, faces like creepy figureheads, teeth and tongues bared. They blocked the path ahead, clawing at the runway. The loser contestants had filled in behind me, a mob. Seeing one way out, I crouched down and slid sideways off the runway, its ragged edge cutting up my thighs and sending pops into the frenzied air. I squeezed through a row of girls to an unused exit, past laughing girls, shocked girls, helpless girls. The door was stuck shut. It needed a whole body to burst it open, but mine was swallowed up, rendered useless inside my mother's clever idea, my ostensible talent, my supreme distinction. I banged as hard as I could with just my fists, pommeling it until it gave way.

Outside on the lawn, I heard the camp director over the microphone.

"Let's settle down, now, boys and girls. Settle down if you want your ice cream."

Wails of disappointment rang out from the rec hall, the next emotional retching, now over dessert rather than me. It had gotten dark, summer dark, feeling like dawn. Feeling out of sequence. I threw my crown onto the grass and ran away from the building, the thump of rubber keeping pace. From behind a tree, I looked back and saw my parents standing outside the door. I watched their arms flail and land on their hips, their spines bend forward, their chins jut. Ice cream dispersed, mouths busy, their words sailed out and rode the air.

"Ridiculous..."

"What you've done…"

"Fault…"

My mother cried and turned away. My father stomped down the hill, shouting my name. A glint of gold paint shot up from the lawn, calling out in the moonlight. From behind the tree, I watched it flicker, the last of the balloons bobbing on my back.

MATCHBOX

Sometimes, I wonder what would happen if Brad's wife died. Early, I mean, not when she became old. It is a terrible thought, I know, but the idea enters my head anyway. It's not that I wish for this to happen, for her to engage a parasite on an overseas trip or suffer a stroke or careen down a mountain on a scooter, because who would ever wish that for another person, particularly someone loved by the person you loved. Or love. Who knows which. Brad told me in one of our phone calls during my divorce that had he not been married, we could be a pair, within seconds. Nanoseconds. So I think about his being married and what an annoyance that is.

Other times, I think that I will just wait until his wife does die. At the natural time. The older time. This is the more respectable way to think, and I feel like a better person thinking about it like this, though it does present an enormous swath of time in which to twiddle one's thumbs. Brad and I will be ninety, maybe. She is of good stock. Hearty. An athletic upper body, I can tell from the holiday cards. At ninety, we will combine households, share toasting ovens and fingertip towels. We will set up framed photos of our children on bookshelves and mantels. We will walk to town, wearing hats. We will be old but will not think that we are.

Meantime, my friend Sally wants me to go on a date with a man she knows. She says that he is the kind of man whom I would like: honest, brainy and handsome. Who wouldn't like a man like that. I know, though, that even honest, brainy and handsome men have needs and wishes that require attention from a woman, should that woman decide to have more to do with him than have a Cobb salad in a restaurant. I am too busy waiting for Brad to deal with all of that, a meal, a second date, an intermingling of any kind, and I think that even talking with this man would simply be unprincipled. Sally says that I should go and just have the salad.

"This is not a moral decision," she tells me.

Sally works with men and farms them out to her friends who actually want to meet them. Plenty of women want to do this. After the fourth time that she mentions it, I agree to go out with the man, Alan. My daughters also urge me to go out with Alan. I'm thinking that they, as teenagers, think that it will be amusing for them if I go through with it, though they insist that the date will be good for me, whatever that means. Good. Insane term.

"And wear a dress," Sally says.

"A what?"

The man has a stunning and tiny car, I can see through the window, not that I care about cars or know about them. But this one is like a baby toy. I don't know how I will fit, and I am quite small.

I open the front door.

"Hello," I say, noting the tan dress pants. Man pants, at a moment squealing for khakis.

"Julia?"

No, Susanna. Wrong house.

I can't figure out how to get into the tiny car. It feels as if I should go head first, like a dive from the side of a pool. I am an incompetent swimmer, and I dive only from the side of a pool, never off the board where the earth sags. I put my left foot on the floor but think it an unwise stretch for my right anterior cruciate ligament and draw it back onto the curb. Alan waits, holding open the door. I smell gardenias, or jasmine, coming from his torso, and a heavy dose at that. One summer, I had a job selling men's accessories in a department store and had whiffed many a sample vial of cologne while no one bought accessories. Alan's scent may have been a hybrid.

"One sec," I say, switching my bag to my other hand and shifting my weight.

"Sit first," he says.

Oh, assistance.

"Then swing your legs in."

I am tempted to end the date there, bent in half, my rear end searching for the seat. I hold onto the roof and the armrest and feel the surface underneath me, finally, grabbing with my third hand onto my head for cover. Fortunately, I don't take Sally's sartorial suggestion and instead, wear jeans. Alan shuts the door and walks around to the driver's side. Positioned so close to the pavement, I can see his calves through the window. In one choreographed and well-honed movement, he curls and swivels his tall body into the seat, contracting involuntarily like a jellyfish or a Martha Graham dancer. To look at him, and his ample midsection, you wouldn't think he'd be able to fold himself and enter his own tiny car so effectively. He must have inhaled to reduce his girth, taken a huge breath on the street before crumpling up. He grabs the wheel, flashing a weighty gold watch and teeth to match his snowy locks. He does have pretty teeth, I must say.

"You all set?" he asks.

I balance my purse on my knees and do not answer his question. My nails are painted the same pink as Brad's wife's nails are, in the New Year's card. I determine the aroma to be the gardenia, after all, the flower of the Mafia. The engine revs up and instantly, the microscopic car zips out into the street. The world seems cockeyed from the passenger seat. My neighbor's house looks purple and misshapen, a home for faeries. The oak canopies now make faces and reach at me. This will be my one and only date with Alan, the Alan who is not Brad, I decide by the end of the block. Not even the end of the block.

OF ALL THINGS

Just because Larry said he had wanted to end his life back in March, and only in March, Sandra could not be sure that the impulse had left him, if he even had one, watching him eat a sandwich three months later. The impetus to commit such an act cannot just wane, she didn't think. Oh, yesterday, I was going to ride my bike off a suspension bridge. Today, I will play cards.

Larry bit into the turkey, and coleslaw dripped out of his mouth. He lurched his head forward so it would hit the plate and not his pants. Coleslaw fluid ran into the latitudinal crease at the top of his chin and branched sideways, tiny tributaries of liquified mayonnaise.

Sandra still didn't love Larry, and that was the reason for his initial desperation. If she had all of a sudden become enamored with him, then, perhaps, his condition could have improved. But she did not, and likely would not. So, she now had two dilemmas with which to contend—what to do about her lack of affection and also, what to do about the threat that that lack of affection and therefore Larry presented to her, their young children and their long-haired Dachshund-poo, Daisy.

Sandra had an internal Peril Index that calculated potential danger innately, thermostatically. She felt it in the lift of a wind, a crinkle of skin, the selection of this word or that.

She met her husband for lunch at Shannahan's that day because it was something that she would have typically done on a workday had she loved him, and she was pressing forward as if this was the case. They had determined not to dissolve their

43

marriage in March simply because Sandra had mentioned that she had no feelings left for Larry, that they had evacuated the places they usually inhabit, the sinews and synapses, the gut. But Larry believed that her feelings could return, somehow. He loved her crazily, and not in the good kind of crazily.

"I want to inhale you," he said once, not understanding that consuming another person would render her invisible, nonexistent, vaporized, and that the person would run from you as if from a whirling vortex.

Sandra knew that her affection would not return, ever, under any circumstance. Larry botched jobs, retold stupid jokes and lost things, all the while pronouncing his sweeping and singular excellence. He took credit for other people's accomplishments and blamed them for his failures. His original *joie de vivre* had crossed that precarious threshold into idiocy. Sandra did not acknowledge to her family or friends that she realized that she had married too quickly and that she had come to think her husband was a cacophonous buffoon. But no one said he wasn't. Everybody knew, except for Larry. Sandra's agreeing to keep her marriage intact was only a temporary decision about which Larry had no idea.

"You know, I was suicidal when you said you didn't love me," he said at the table before the coleslaw spilled from his lip.

It was the first Sandra had heard of it.

"The doctor gave me medication, so I'm good now."

She rested her fork on the edge of the salad bowl.

Her Peril Index went berserk at Larry's revelation. She did not know that Larry saw a psychiatrist when she told him she didn't love him. Larry led an emotional life outside the realm of their emotional life, and Sandra knew that she'd have to stay in the marriage past the time she had forecasted, the point at which her children were old enough to communicate on their own if they were left with him in an emergency. Now, she'd have to stay until they couldn't be endangered by anything that Larry might do. God knows how old they'd have to be for that.

Betsy Wingate's father asphyxiated himself with fumes from his Plymouth Reliant when Sandra and Betsy were in fourth grade. He went into the garage at night. Betsy, Sandra's best friend, came back to school a week later. She stepped tepidly afterward, and her knee socks rose to different heights, something that they didn't do before the incident. Sandra walked Betsy home each day after school and made sure she got inside and took off her jacket and put her notebooks down on the shelf by the kitchen. She understood the magnitude of such loss and the care it required.

"How were you going to do it?" Sandra asked, incensed and skeptical, but not showing it.

"That's what you want to know?"

Larry had a heightened sense of smell, so he would not have used Mr. Wingate's method. He would not have wanted to be so stimulated, olfactorily. He would not have leaped from anything, either, as that would have required planning, and Larry was impulsive, tearing out of the house with faucets running and lights on, interrupting people because he couldn't wait to say what he was thinking or didn't know how long the thought would remain in his head for the grabbing. He probably would have driven into headlights. He would have been entranced by the rumble of the road, the shooting of the glare past him, comets in a black sky. It would have felt cinematic.

Sandra took a bite of her chicken salad. Shannahan's made it with the tarragon, which she particularly enjoyed and couldn't duplicate at home. Sandra suspected that Larry was inventing the story to make her worry and want to care for him, trifling with something so grave for his own purposes. It would be like him to do something so heinous. When she wouldn't have sex with him, he threatened her with single motherhood. That is not the way to get someone to have sex with you. But Larry studied drama in college and was adept at delivering lines, evoking responses in the audience. He never made it as an actor, probably because that's all he did, say the words without knowing why the character said them or who the character was. Larry had no patience for such work.

He asked again. "That's what you want to know? Of all things?"

"You volunteered this information," Sandra said. "Headlights?"

Larry threw the turkey sandwich onto his plate. His fingers dripped from the tips. He scraped his chair backwards to look for his napkin, which had fallen to the floor earlier in the meal. He lurched to snatch it and bounced up like a child's punching bag, flushed red like a goofy dinosaur. A translucent trickle of slaw juice remained on his chin, and Sandra motioned to hers, to let him know. Then, she called the waiter over and asked him to pack up the rest of her lunch.

She went back to her office but returned home earlier than usual that afternoon. She let the babysitter leave and checked on her children, who were napping in their beds. In the bathroom, Sandra scoured Larry's medicine cabinet, twisting around the amber vials to read the names of the drugs. Larry had a few non-threatening conditions—high cholesterol, migraine—so he always had a collection of vials on the shelf, the contents of which Sandra had studied when they were first prescribed. But she found three unfamiliar containers, fat ones for jumbo pills. She sat them on the counter and wrote down the names of the medications and physicians, along with the dosage for each. Knowing that her children would soon be waking up, she quickly returned the vials to the cabinet, ran downstairs to her computer and researched her findings.

One drug treated anxiety; another, high blood pressure; and the third, depression. Severe depression. Take-your-own-life depression. While the anxiety and high blood pressure were new ailments, and concerning in their own right, Sandra focused for obvious reasons on the last diagnosis. She sensed something askew, and not from what she was reading. She picked up a paperweight in her palm and closed her eyes. Upstairs in the bathroom, the physical weight of the third vial had registered in her hand.

"Too heavy," she whispered to herself at her desk.

Daisy at her heels, she tore back up the steps, down the hall, into the bathroom. She snatched the vial from the cabinet. "One tablet per day."

She checked the date: "March 16, 2016."

The number of doses: "90."

The expired days: Seventy-six.

Fourteen pills should have remained in the bottle, had Larry been taking them as prescribed, had Larry been, in truth, curing his desire to self-destruct, if he in fact had such a desire. Sandra

46

took the bottle into her closet, a roomy space where she went sometimes to be alone. She sat on the floor and spilled the tablets into a shoebox, shuttling them to its opposite side as she counted. They hit the cardboard with a *tic* and wobbled.

Total: Eighty-eight.

With two hands, she held the box of jiggling pills and stood, staring at their gall, their deceit, their presumption, her skirts and dresses and jeans a backdrop. Purses lined up, for evening, for summer, for fall. Shoes, heel to heel. On the carpet, an alphabet book and zoo animal puzzle. A basket of capes and tutus, cowboy hats and wands.

Sandra tilted the box, and the pills thundered into a corner. She poured them back into the vial, snapped the lid shut and headed for the bathroom. But she stopped before leaving the closet. From the top drawer of a dresser, she took a pair of socks and separated them. Into one, she slid the vial, pushing it to the end and balling it up in the other, out of view. She returned it to the drawer and hid it, under the other socks, a scarf snagged off a hook, a winter hat. Having taken just the two pills, Larry would not miss the bottle in his medicine cabinet. Sandra sensed that she might need to have it, not right then, but later. For something, she didn't know what. She opened the drawer again and pushed the container as far back as it could go.

In the bathroom, she spaced out the other two bottles on the shelf, filling the void. She looked at herself in the mirror, washed her hands with soap, tied up her hair in a knot.

It was time for the children to wake up. She walked down the hall to rouse them, pausing against their door, steadying herself before entering. Inside the room, she pulled open the curtains and stacked up the books and tidied up the toys. "Mommy's home," she said, stroking their heads. "Let's have some fun."

BEHIND THE WHEEL

A ndrew and his father sat in the Chevy Suburban, waiting for the men to come out with Grandmother Maureen. They figured she'd be wheeled from the building, but the cart was in use, so the men carried her instead. Grandmother Maureen was six-foot-two, even at ninety. Not one to shrink. They needed an extra guy.

"She's coming," said Andrew, jumping out to open the trunk. His father followed. "Jesus, Dad, golf clubs? And the banjo?"

Hank reached in and shoved his belongings to the side. The men slid the casket into the sports utility vehicle and pushed it until it hit the back of the passenger seat.

"I knew she'd fit," said Hank, Grandmother Maureen's first-born.

It is expensive to hire a hearse to drive a body 560 miles, across state lines. Hank was a proficient saver and master recycler, reusing the foil from sticks of gum, even. And since he sidelined as the Clark County Medical Examiner, he was legally permitted to transport a dead person in his car. His wife, thinking that such a road trip was ill-advised, not to mention gruesome, refused to accompany him. So, he enlisted Andrew as co-pilot for the eight-hour drive from Arkadelphia, Arkansas to San Antonio.

"It's a nice coffin," said Andrew, swiveling in the front seat. "Flashy."

"Your mother picked it."

Hank Gallagher had a history of speeding, the kind of speeding that would have earned citations and fines and license confiscations if not for his governmental appointment and the leniency of law enforcement officers, many of whom Hank treated in his internal medicine practice. As Chief of Emergency Medicine at the regional hospital, he was accustomed to calling the shots, particularly those under pressure. He had witnessed thousands of accidents—vehicular and not—so his complicated relationship with speed confounded his family, friends and, of course, highway patrol.

Three years before Grandmother Maureen died, Hank had swerved a previous Chevy Suburban to avoid a suitcase in his lane and wound up strewn on the pavement with half his scalp ten feet from his head. His dog, Pilot, was ejected and found later on the side of the road, upright and unscathed. Mighty auspicious, that name.

Hank accelerated out of the funeral home parking lot and ripped through the yellow light at the corner. Andrew tightened his belt.

Grandmother Maureen was an heiress to a Texan steel fortune and the matriarch of the family. She married a World War II bomber and had the disposition to be one herself. For most of her life, she oversaw Fredericksburg Metals Inc., and she raised three sons, two of whom became physicians and the third, a rancher.

"Next time, take a lesson from that clever dog of yours," she said to Hank following the accident.

Andrew felt the casket press up into the back of his seat. With slight shifts in velocity, the pressure on his thoracic vertebra increased and receded, curving his spine forward and back like a reed at the beach. After an hour, Andrew became concerned that if his father hit something in the road, again, Grandmother Maureen would plow through his midsection at ninety-two miles per hour, her inertia ransacking his spleen, lungs, abdomen. Everything. Quietly, he unlatched his belt, gambling that he stood a better shot at survival being catapulted like Pilot through the windshield than strapped in and mowed down. It was a risky and also morbid dilemma to have en route to your grandmother's funeral, but it was not the first fraught choice his family had presented. Ripped your meniscus and lost the soccer scholarship? Join the army or pay your own way. Your wife colluded with your business partner and stole your company? Get a new company.

Andrew braced his feet on the floorboard. After two hours, the carburetor light lit up, and Hank pulled off the road to find a gas station. Andrew's hips ached.

"Let's hope there's a mechanic," said Hank.

"Let's hope he only looks under the hood," said Andrew.

"You boys quit carrying on," Grandmother Maureen thought.

They got out of the car, and Hank locked the doors with the remote. The windows were tinted, fortunately. Arkadelphia sun. It was noon, and they were due at the funeral home in San Antonio by seven. The ceremony was scheduled for the next afternoon. At Hank's rate of speed, they'd make it by five, if not earlier.

A man walked out of the garage and nodded hello.

"What's her trouble?" he asked.

"Carburetor," said Hank, popping up the hood.

Andrew wiped his forehead.

"Turn her on, will ya?" the mechanic asked.

Hank hopped in behind the wheel, with vigor, as if a dead parent did not lay behind him in a flashy coffin. Andrew distracted the mechanic with chit-chat.

"Sweet shop you've got here," he said. "Family business?"

"Yep, Grand-daddy's, been here since the thirties," said the mechanic, knocking around. "All right," he waved to Hank, pulling down the hood. "She's got a bum carburetor. Needs a new one."

"Can I make it to San Antonio?" Hank asked.

"The San Antonio three blocks from here, maybe," said the mechanic, laughing.

"How long to put it in?"

"Not long, if I had one."

"You don't have one?"

"Hang on."

The mechanic went into the garage. He didn't hurry.

"We should get her out of the sun, Dad."

"Hooray for Hollywood," Grandmother Maureen thought.

The man came back with an employee, whom he sent somewhere in a pick-up to retrieve the new carburetor. Meantime, Hank drove the Chevy Suburban around the side of the garage, into the shade and out of view. He took his banjo out of the trunk and picked the strings. "Rhinestone Cowboy." Then, he sang.

Hank was a bad singer.

"You doing okay?" Andrew asked.

"We'll get there in time," Hank said in between phrases. "I'm not worried."

"Not that."

"What then?" Hank dampened the strings. "Look, son. Pneumonia at that age is tough. They can't fight it, the older patients."

Hank switched to John Denver. "Rocky Mountain High." He strained to reach the notes.

Andrew shook his head and paced in the driveway on the side of the garage. "Well, she was right about Stacy."

"Which part?"

"She told me at the wedding to keep my bank accounts to myself and not have any babies. Then she said to 'go dance and have fun.'"

"Sounds about right."

"What?"

"We weren't surprised. Your mother and I never trusted her. And your brother predicted the whole thing."

"Are you serious?"

"Why wouldn't I be serious? You can't tell a kid everything."

"A little something, though. You can tell a kid *something*."

From Hank's vantage point on the curb, he noticed a wet spot on the ground underneath the car. Soon, he saw dripping. A weekend tinkerer, he didn't think that auto parts utilizing liquid were positioned in the midsection of a vehicle. He put down the banjo and knelt next to the door.

"She's leaking," Hank said, bolting up.

"That's probably normal in a carburetor."

"Not the car!"

Andrew ran around the side of the Chevy and dropped to his stomach.

"Touch it to make sure," Hank said.

"Are you out of your mind? I'm not touching it."

"Move over, then. Christ."

Hank stretched his arm under the Chevy Suburban and tapped his hand into the wet patch. He sat on the pavement and rubbed his fingers together, analyzing the texture. Then, he sniffed them at their tips.

"Formaldehyde. Look," he said, shooting his hand forward. "Sloppy work. Must have been the new guy."

Andrew jumped back, grabbing his stomach.

They determined that when the carburetor arrived, Hank would drive the car around to the shop and Andrew would hover over the spot, blocking the puddle from view. The last thing they wanted was for the mechanic to think something else was awry and begin investigating. Mechanics like to find extra trouble. Meanwhile, they flanked the vehicle in case another customer came by.

"You know, you told me to settle down already," Andrew said. "'Enough dating,' that's what you told me. Sitting on your patio, clear as day."

"I did, you're right."

"You gave me a deadline."

"Exactly. You had time to pick the right girl. Not the first girl."

Andrew, now thirty-eight, was two years old when Hank married his mother and adopted him. His biological father took off before he was born and moved to Georgia with another woman. Andrew's mom, thinking he'd only cause havoc, told him to stay away, and he did. At the proper time, she told Andrew about the circumstances of his birth. When he was twenty-three, he got a call from the man, Chris, who asked to see him. It took a few requests, but Andrew agreed to meet him one time. He didn't tell his parents, thinking they'd feel bad. His mother and Hank had two kids after him, neither of whom was as intelligent or athletic or as good-natured as Andrew.

He rested his hand on Grandmother Maureen's window. "You pushed me, Dad. Hard. Not like Ali and Rich. You still do."

Hank took some steps and scratched the back of his neck. "I wasn't thrilled that your mother had you, I'll be straight. I was on call every other night, at the hospital for days at a time and making no money, and now a kid running around. No handouts from that one, either." He tilted his head toward the car. "Know what she said?"

Andrew combed his fingers through his dark hair and crossed his arms.

"Give him your damn name, and crucify him if he ever cheats on a woman."

Andrew took it in. "Sounds about right."

"It was right," Hank said, gripping his son's shoulder. "Bless her soul."

Andrew paced by the side of the vehicle. He skimmed his fingers along the white racing stripe. "I met him once, you know. Chris, I met him. Fifteen years ago."

"Down in Atlanta, I know. The bastard called the house, and let's just say it was a good thing I answered." Hank leaned his back up against the car and closed his eyes. "Don't worry, your mother has no idea."

"He said he wouldn't tell you."

Hank laughed. "Nothing since then, I figure."

"Nothing."

After nearly three hours, the repair had been made. Hank blasted the air conditioner and flew out of the parking lot at high speed, warranted this time. They arrived in San Antonio past seven p.m., but the funeral home director agreed to accept Grandmother Maureen despite the hour, particularly given Hank's medical description of her tumescence, or lack thereof.

By the next afternoon, she had been hydrated—and with additional milliliters, just in case. A tough one, Grandmother Maureen showed no sign of having been derailed or dried out.

"Fantastic," Hank said. "She looks fantastic."

"Damn straight," Grandmother Maureen thought.

In the chapel, Hank sat with his wife to the left, and Andrew, Ali and Rich to the right. Andrew turned each way, seeing the Gallagher chin ripple down the row, the blond hair glow violet and blue in the stained glass. The minister walked to the podium while the choir sang, and Hank straightened up on the bench, humming the tune of the hymn. Off key and a beat behind, he tapped his hand on Andrew's knee. The music soared to the rafters, and the service began.

SHADELAND

The way it works, people go into the store looking for new shades for their old lamps. They plant their feet and bend their knees and wrench open the door with one hand, the other gripping the fixture by its neck or cradling it on a stomach. Sometimes, the shade has disintegrated from its frame, or it has faded from sitting in a window. Sometimes, customers want to switch a lamp from one room to another and need a new style to suit the decor. Some need the lamp to perform a different function, to become a reading lamp, say, after a life as a subtle diffuser. You cannot have the same shade to read and to diffuse. The people usher the lamps carefully, with reverence, banners of their particular rite of passage. A woman whose last baby has gone to college, converting his room into a study. A man whose wife is confined to bed, needing a brighter beam on her needlepoint. Aunt Trudy's estate, divvied up.

Alice has re-entered the workforce, taking a job at the store, Shadeland. A name that makes you grin. Of course, what else. Shadeland sells just the shades, no lamps. At least six times a day, people come in wanting to buy lamps, and Alice tells them that they don't sell the lamps, that they sell the shades, only.

"Try Lighting Alley, down the street," she says, six times a day. "No, not in the alley, on the street."

Alice taught school for twenty-seven years and had just retired when Walter, her husband, became ill. They were planning to spend more time together, after decades of third-graders and spelling tests, but that didn't happen. The house was big and hollow. She would have to move, but she didn't know where to. The store was a place to go, meantime.

The customers set down their lamps and tell their stories to Alice. She puts on her glasses to examine the lamps and make suggestions and takes them off to listen to the people. She looks sad sometimes, nodding her head, touching her chest, and she smiles, saying things that make the people grab her hand or hug her across the table. She tells all of her customers about Walter, about how he doesn't like leaves on the porch, how he savors pistachio in a sugar cone, lets his tie fly in the wind. In a few short months on the job, Alice becomes an expert in finials and proper neck lengths, harps and shade-to-height proportion, and also human transitions and hardships. The people come to the store many times before deciding on their purchases, carrying the lamps back and forth from home. Badges. Emblems of the circumstance, the shift. Alice continues the conversation each time, about the base circumference, the grade of silk, the empty closet now, the full closet, still. Alice is the lamp therapist and the metaphor is banal, the holder of the light, the vessel for sight, clarity. Seeming to be illuminated, but really in the dark as much as they.

Don't do anything important for a while, she was advised when Walter died. Don't make decisions about anything except what you will have for dinner. Decide on the chicken or the oatmeal, but nothing else. And it is okay to have the oatmeal, if that is what you want, if that is what your body tells you to eat, if that is where your hand reaches inside the cabinet. Let it just reach where it wants; let it just happen on its own. Add a banana. Don't add a banana. Just don't pack and move to a houseboat or give away your money or adopt a baby.

———————

One afternoon, a woman enters the store holding a pink candlestick lamp, medium size, with glass spheres interspersed through the wood. The woman's sister is coming to live with her in an apartment over the garage, and she will use the lamp, which is being switched from a daughter's room. It has a pink and green polka-dotted shade, and pom-poms line the lower edge. The finial is a ballet dancer. A toe shoe hangs from the on-off chain. The woman plans to remove the ballerina and the toe shoe and replace them with standard parts.

"You must keep this as is," Alice says to the woman. "You mustn't touch it."

"It's cute, I know," the woman says.

Alice circles slowly around the table, entranced. "It's more than that." She slides one leg in front of the other.

The woman insists that it is the only spare lamp in the house, and that her daughter has moved out and left it there.

Alice stops walking. "Did your daughter dance?"

"For a minute. Hated it and quit."

Alice recoils. "But a grandchild?"

The daughter has boys, and she has lamps with baseball bats and no, she is not going to keep the dancing lamp as a dancing lamp. It is not a consideration.

Alice shakes her head. Her earrings jiggle.

"Can we please just find a shade for it?" the woman asks.

Alice pushes the sleeves of her sweater to her forearms, still lean and graceful. Slowly, she moves the lamp to the center of the table and takes off the polka-dotted shade, exposing the harp and the socket, both the original parts. "From the fifties, yes?"

The woman shrugs and checks her watch.

The base is intricately carved, with narrowings and collars on both sides of the glass orbs.

"The facets are beautiful, so delicate," Alice says, tilting the lamp by the neck to catch the light. "The modern ones are bigger and reflect nothing, just for show."

She pulls the toe shoe and smiles. Traces her finger over the dancer's arabesque. Steps back.

"Well?" the woman says.

Alice positions the polka-dotted shade back on the lamp and attaches the finial, spinning the dancer carefully. A pirouette. And another.

"I'm just going to slap some white paint on it, so maybe a plain shade and one of these things for the top," the woman says, snatching an all-purpose metal ball from a basket by the register.

Alice flinches.

She danced when she was younger, all through her childhood and even after having her sons, now grown and plane rides away. For a birthday, maybe her ninth or tenth, her parents bought her a baby blue case for her leotard and tights, outfitted with a slipper compartment that snapped shut. Alice thought that the separate chamber was remarkable, for her slippers to be treasured so. She stored them carefully, smoothing them out and pressing them together sole to sole before securing them inside, retrieving them the next time as if extracting gold from a safe. She hung the ballet case on her shoulder and was instantly transformed, her torso lengthening, hips tucking and turn-out widening. She felt part of something exceptional.

Alice stands behind the lamp and lifts it up with two hands. "I'll take it out back and work on some possibilities. When do you need it?"

"I really just want to pick one and take it home today."

"Oh, but it's not that easy, and I've got some customers ahead of you. How about Friday?"

The woman leaves, and Alice takes the ballet lamp to the back of the workroom, where she places it last in the queue.

"Looks like a period piece," her manager says.

"Awaiting destruction."

"Ah, one of those. Criminal."

At closing time, it's Alice's turn to lock up. She does it quickly, not liking to be alone in the store. Shadeland is situated in a busy suburban shopping center, but by evening, the foot traffic slows. She secures the top and bottom locks on the front door, flips the Open sign and heads to the rear exit, where she shuts all but the night lights and grabs her coat. The manager insists that his employees park in the back lot, reserving the spots in front for customers. The lot is well lit, and at six p.m., salespeople from other stores are leaving en masse, so Alice feels safe enough. Two doors down, there is a pizza place that stays open until nine, and on Fridays, she treats herself to dinner. The guys in the shop know her, and they know that she will order chicken marsala, spaghetti and a side salad, with Roquefort dressing, which she will take home. There is enough for Saturday, too. No one orders the Roquefort, the men tell her.

Alice puts on her coat and ties her scarf. She is about to set the alarm system but hesitates. Across the room, the customers' lamps are lined up on a shelf, their original shades now gone. Their harps sit like heads, faceless, brainless, hairless, but full of shape. Oval, round, elongated. Under them, the bodies, some squat and rotund, the ginger jars. Slim and tapered, the columns. Curvaceous, the gourds. They are spectators in the stands. Theatre-goers in their seats. The dancing lamp is the last, at the end of the row. Perfectly proportioned, demure but sturdy. Without forethought, Alice whisks across the room and reaches up to take hold of its base, rising into an élevé, her back foot in coup-de-pied. She plucks it off the shelf, spins like Clara with the Nutcracker, and sashays out the door. Exit stage left.

Mail still arrives for Walter. Alice takes it in and puts it on his desk. In a hall closet, she finds a small frosted bulb and screws it into the dancing lamp, which she places on the kitchen table. The chicken marsala steams from the tin. An extra container of the Roquefort is hidden in the bag. Alice smiles. On Fridays, she pours herself a glass of red wine, chianti, and she uses the wedding china. Royal Copenhagen's Blue Half Lace, chosen for its flouted rim. She and Walter shopped for it together at an antique shop in the Berkshires. The other dishes, with their smooth and serious edges, were no match for the whimsical scallops. Alice sits at the table, takes the toe shoe in her fingers and pulls the chain.

She and Walter met in their twenties at an outdoor concert in Western Massachusetts. Students, they were each working at summer jobs. He spotted her across the lawn and took nearly an hour to migrate her way.

"This is a big lawn," he said, before saying hello.

"One of the biggest," she replied.

Piano music plays from the stereo system in the living room. Alice gets lost in a fugue, its thematic variations sweeping her one after the other deeper into the piece. Her head sways. An arm extends to the side, its hand opening. A welcome. A preparation. She pours a second glass of wine.

Later, Alice takes the lamp upstairs and sets it on a table in her bedroom, next to an overstuffed chair. She changes into one of Walter's flannel shirts and flops down with a book. Used to be, she sat there to feed the boys their bottles, to read to them, to mark her school papers. To review the work day with Walter, and more recently, to check on him as he napped. A chair with purpose. Accountability. Now, it is hers alone, and it demands nothing.

Alice pulls the lamp chain and opens the book. She reads a page and picks up the phone, checking the time before dialing. It's too late to call Peter, but only seven o'clock at Stuart's house.

"We're good, just getting to be bath time," he says. "How's the store?"

"The same," Alice says, tapping the toe shoe, watching it swing. "Is my grandbaby walking all over town by now?"

"She's running. I can't keep up."

"That's wonderful. Soon she'll be leaping the fences."

Stuart's wife calls for him from down the hall.

"Hey, Mom, got to run the bath."

"Go, go, sweetheart. It's okay."

Alice begins dialing Peter's number but stops and puts down the phone. She closes the book and flips on the TV. The corner of the room warms in the glow of the lamp. A shadow of the toe shoe moves across the table and back, stretching into an exquisite point each time. Alice lays her head back, tired. The cushion, worn and reliable, envelops her head, contains it, lets it wander. To the barre, to the music on the Massachusetts lawn, to her babies in their cribs. She pulls her blanket to her neck, curls to the side and sleeps.

STRAY

"This will be where you will stay," the nun said, leading me into a room. She showed me how to operate the thermostat and jiggle the shower drain, kneeling down and reaching into the floor of the tub. Her veil lay flat on the center of her back, sliding nowhere despite the bending and stretching and twisting. "It's a finicky one, dear."

I pushed the curtain over and stood to her right to watch.

"You have to pull up more than you think and give it a good yank, like this," said the nun, looking up at me, pressing her lips together, concentrating. Her one cheek squeezed out of the white casing around her face—the wimple, it's called, fantastically, I later found out. I thought that a nun in a wimple would be doing more ethereal things, more incomprehensible and uncomfortably mystical things, as Rabbi Epstein did in Sunday School when I was eleven. So glad I was that Mom and Dad let me off the Hebraic hook after my brother was bar mitzvahed. Not to worry, I wasn't converting or anything, or relinquishing my religious heritage, dotted though it was with atheists, God bless them. I simply needed to rent a room. And Our Lady of Peace had just what I wanted.

I unpacked my suitcases, slipped on jammies and hopped into bed, which I had remade with linens I brought to Philadelphia from New York. The room was entirely taupe. The walls, moldings, curtains, floor...all taupe. Without my rosebud-covered quilt and shams, it would have been difficult to tell where the carpet ended and the mattress began.

I lay down under the cross and gazed up at the infinitesimal

Jesus. "Hello," I said.

I had not slept under a Jesus before, being Jewish. In fact, my father didn't like any objects hanging over our beds for fear they would loosen from their hooks and tumble onto our skulls. Even if we weren't Jewish, Jesus would have had to suspend from a less precarious spot in my room, or at least a place under which I was generally alert.

"The quilt helps," I said. "You think?"

He didn't answer. So diminutive he was, microbial almost, my own small fry Jesus. His fingers were the size of ice cream sprinkles.

I grabbed the taupe flashlight on the nightstand and stood up on the bed to see, face to face with the bantamweight icon. I illuminated the full length of his body, noticing the fine musculature. He had a long-distance runner's physique, like the crew captain I pined for in chemistry class, the one at the lab table by the window, lit up brilliantly one day, moody and subdued the next. A vessel of nature.

"You're dusty," I said. "Come here."

I stretched down the cuff of my pajama top and gently wiped his shoulders and arms, where most of the dirt had settled. Then, I blew on his feet.

"You could really use a bath, you know," I told Jesus, "and maybe a nice seaweed facial." I pictured my new roomie floating in the sink in the in-quarters bathroom at the Our Lady of Peace Catholic rooming house, sudsed up with cleanser.

Tucked back into bed, I prepared, mentally, for the next day, yet another stepping stone in my burgeoning television career. I would be a production assistant at a network affiliate, a lowly job, but a job in a Top Ten market. The News Director could not commit to a full-time position, but he was able to hire me on a month-by-month basis. Hence, the determination to camp out at the church, which did not require a year-long lease. I decided to call Jesus, Jee, for short.

––––––––

It was my intention, actually, not to spend too much time at Our Lady, as Geoffrey lived just minutes away in a townhouse with futons and blond wood furniture from the forties. Interesting that I should recognize his toxicity yet yearn to be with him from dawn to dusk, permitting him to readjust my belts, retie my pony-tails, reconstruct my sentences, redo, or try to, whatever could be redone. He might have rechopped a carrot, if it were possible. But oh, the glory that was Geoffrey P. Jamison.

Introduced to me at an art opening a summer earlier when I was twenty-three, Geoffrey sparred immediately and invited me out afterward for pierogies at an East Village coffee shop, to be shared, as is the custom, with one fork. Or so he said. Blondness pervaded him and was mesmerizing, as it had become apparent by that point in my psycho-social-sexual development that I possessed a preferred boy tint.

Geoffrey's ideal nature made me idiotic. I could handle defect, but flawlessness left me stumped. On our second date, we ate Ethiopian beef with our hands, which I hated but said I loved. On our third date, we watched a Pakistani film that I loved but said I hated. After a month more of such nonsense, we each went elsewhere and the dating ceased.

We ran into each other on the Madison Avenue bus just before I left for Our Lady. Geoffrey was in town for the weekend. I had chosen to stand, and while holding the strap, I felt a tugging on my shoulder bag. Thinking that a fellow passenger was pick-pocketing my wallet, I snapped my head around and assumed the defensive stance. Geoffrey was sitting a row behind, leaning forward to reach me.

"Hey, you, come sit."

"It's you, how *are* you?" I said, fixing my bangs. "I thought you were robbing me."

The bus stopped and the woman behind him got up.

"Quick, grab this one."

Stardust danced around his head.

The bus took off with a jolt, and I catapulted into the seat. Grace eluded me around Geoffrey P. Jamison. I could do split leaps on the balance beam. People commented on my carriage and stride. But within a hundred-yard radius of this person, I was a spastic mess, tripping, tangling up in cords, my nose running like a neglected toddler.

"Ow," said the woman next to me.

"I'm sorry," I sniffled. "He took off so fast."

"He took off so fast, didn't he?" I repeated to Geoffrey. The woman scowled and pulled her purse to her chest.

"You need to anticipate better, Sam."

On our second date, Geoffrey taught me how to jostle shoulders on pedestrian-filled streets. It's a sort of shimmy, right shoulder forward, then left, then right. Suburban girls don't know about it, and city boys are arrogant, but suburban girls love them and therefore, let them teach them how to do things like walk. Show me how to walk, Geoffrey. Please. I forgot. Next, we'll do the skipping.

On the bus, Geoffrey said that he was working in Philadelphia, the very Philadelphia where I was headed. I told him I'd be at Our Lady, and he said that we should get together.

"I knew someone who stayed there," he said.

"It's short-term."

"And that's good."

Good, for him, was he thinking? Good that I'd be short-term, not long-term, not a girlfriend, but a date with someone he dated in the past, if he'd even ask me? Or good for me, somehow, that my tenure at a church rooming house would be swift, that it's not the kind of spot in which a young media professional should remain beyond a certain period of time.

"Yes, very good," I agreed, to what I didn't know.

"This is my stop," Geoffrey said, zipping up his leather bomber jacket with the raspberry lining.

"Love that."

"Got it in the Village. It's vintage." He ringed a scarf around his neck ninety-two times, like a halo. It made me feel warm. Too warm, maybe. Sick, really. I felt sick.

"Great to see you, Samantha. Let's catch up when you get to town."

"You, too, and yes, let's do that. The catching. Let's."

He laughed, in a patronizing, infantilizing and beautiful way that made his eyelashes turn up and sunshine glow from beneath his skin. The bus screeched to a halt, inertia lost on Geoffrey P. Jamison, the highly trained bus rider extraordinaire. And he was gone. Onto 49th Street, shedding dazzle and doubt into the lives of others.

I flopped again into the woman.

"Ughhh," she said, pushing me off her shoulder.

———————

To receive phone calls at Our Lady of Peace, one had to first go through Our Lady at the Desk, Miss Mary. Miss Mary of pen and pad and teeth, so many teeth in her lovely head, capped, like a nurse, but not a nun. There were no telephones in the individual rooms, so when a call came in, it would go to the phone on Miss Mary's desk in the lobby. She would answer it, saying, "Good afternoon. Christ is Lord." Or, "Good morning or evening. Christ is Lord." The caller would ask to speak with a certain resident, and Miss Mary would say, "I will leave her a message that you pho-o-o-ned," stretching out the long "o" as they do in Baltimore. Later, maybe nineteen hours later, a square of green paper would be taped to your door. Printed on top was a line drawing of a ringing phone, with the zig-zags spraying out from the receiver, like perspiration drops from a cartoon athlete. Underneath would be the name and number of the caller, written in fanciful cursive.

I returned from the TV station one evening to find such a note. There it was, Geoffrey Jamison, 215.545.3991. My oh my. As simple as that. A frame, perhaps, maybe silver. This was, as I analyzed it, the zenith of my boy arc. The crest, the corona of all amassed experience. I untaped the paper from the door and took it inside.

"Hey Jee, wait 'till you see this."

I wondered if Geoffrey knew how clumsy I felt at the Ethiopian restaurant and at every other place I went with him. It was generous and worldly of him not to rule me out entirely just because I was inept back then, if he thought I was. How could he not have thought I was. A tribute to good parenting, I suppose. A mother who typed Braille on East 82nd Street, a father who volunteered at Legal Aid. They had raised Geoffrey to give a girl a chance. I liked them very much, though I had never met them and in all likelihood, never would. I'd have brought them a box of teas and maybe some imported honey. That would have been a lovely and appropriate gift.

Males were not permitted beyond the Our Lady lobby, so I waited for Geoffrey downstairs. Miss Mary watched from her chair, manning telecommunications. "Good evening. Christ is Lord."

"Hey," Geoffrey smiled, coming through the door. "Nice lobby."

"The nicest," I agreed. "Bye, Miss Mary."

"I will leave her a message that you ph-o-o-ned," she said into the receiver, nodding in my direction. Miss Mary did not approve of Geoffrey, I could tell.

"I was thinking Italian," he said, brushing back his hair while we walked around the corner. "Hop on."

"What?"

He handed me a helmet.

"Just tuck your hair in back," he said, tucking my hair in back.

"Geoffrey, I do not think I can get on a motorcycle."

"It's not a real motorcycle. It's a BMW."

"I can't. My father would kill me."

Geoffrey secured the helmet on my head. "We're only going ten blocks, on city streets."

"I can't. I just can't."

"Don't worry, I'll go slowly. Just wrap your arms around my waist."

Wrap your arms around my waist.

The words drifted in the air like cherubs amongst the clouds.

Slay me now, I am finished. Boy and girl on a bike, girl clinging to boy for protection, grasping with desire, abandoning all to the pilot of her heart. My father will absolutely murder me. I will be a dead girl with desire. I get on. He revs up. I clutch him and gasp.

Penne pomodoro. And escarole.

———————

During my five months in Philadelphia, I proceeded down this risky road, Against My Better Judgment Road. Geoffrey and I went on dates, maybe one every week and a half. We had a common appreciation for aesthetics and the creative process, except that his appreciation was, of course, better than mine. We listened to music, went to museums, had picnics, bought vests. I was thrilled to have this particular boy on my arm, though I felt as if I was in the wrong gym, able to manage one back handspring when the others could do four.

"Jee," I confessed one night in the dark. "I don't feel like myself around this boy. I mean, I rehearse the words before I say them. That can't be good. Is that bad, Jee? Is that bad?"

I went on. "If you liked someone, say, someone teeny and wooden and available, but you felt that she would judge everything you did, and so you acted only to please her, wouldn't that make you feel stupid?"

I lay on my back and thought about what I had asked. "I think it would make you feel stupid, Jee. I really do."

I snatched the flashlight and shined it at him, extending my arms overhead like a teepee.

"I can't do it anymore. He has to like me for me," I said. "Thank you, Jee. You're the best."

———————

Geoffrey had cats. And the cats had kittens, whom I feared. They slept on Geoffrey's head, and ultimately on mine, on the occasional night I stayed over. Two-pound fur-puffs with sharp nails, incisors and schemes in their brains. I could not sleep with felines on my crown, but to toss them onto the floor would risk offending the slumbering boy of wonder. So I let the kitties repose on my coif, remaining awake, the circles under my eyes darkening with each passing hour.

By six a.m., the bird would rise. Its cage was a handsome antique, curled iron and white. The bird was verbally advanced and psychotic, probably because of its roommates. Truman, his name was. Good morning, Truman. Shut your despicable mouth, Truman.

Geoffrey was like Tarzan in his own wild kingdom, at one with the creatures. You are me, I am you, scratch my beard, eat my Corn Flakes. It was annoying from a lifestyle perspective, but I must say, it was really attractive.

The Saturday before my stint at the station was over and I was to return to New York, a stray dog appeared at the back door while we were listening to Geoffrey sing. Sensing fraternity, he had found its way to the house, like a lost soul to nondenominational worship.

"Look," I exclaimed, in between the "Hey" and "Jude."

Geoffrey spun around on the piano stool.

"Look. A dog, a really cute dog."

"Oh him."

"You know him?"

"He's come around a few times."

The dog, a mid-size terrier/collie/spaniel mutt, was so happy when I opened the door, and he walked right inside. I rubbed his ears and let him sniff me. He was all ribs beneath the fur, so we gave him some turkey and a few pieces of carrot.

"I think you should take him with you," Geoffrey said a little while later.

"Where?"

"Home to New York. He should be adopted, and I can't keep him here, with the cats."

"You have a bird with the cats."

"Just take him. Look, he loves you."

"I'm going to my parents' house first, on Amtrak. There is absolutely no way I can take him."

Two days later, I had the cab stop off at Geoffrey's house en route to the train station. I had bid Jee and Miss Mary adieu, thanking them both for their hospitality and Jee, individually, for being such a good listener.

"They'll be others," I told him, "but I'm your favorite, I know."

Before leaving, I took one of Miss Mary's green papers from the trash. "Don't forget to dust me!" I wrote, and then tucked it behind Jee's neck. I jumped off the bed but had a second thought and jumped back on. "Bless you," I added at the bottom.

Geoffrey had taken Flash to the vet for a check-up, bathed him and bought a lime green collar and leash. They were waiting for me on the front step.

"You guys look so cozy up there," I said, getting out of the taxi. "You sure you don't want to stay, Flash?"

Please say you want to stay, Flash. Please. I grasped the

imprudence of what I was about to do. There was not a sensible argument for taking the dog to New York. I relinquished all reason for a boy, a boy who made me feel shaky, a boy who probably wouldn't call again, whether I adopted the mutt or not.

Geoffrey dropped the leash and the dog, my dog, came running, jumping on me and kissing, the way I wanted Geoffrey to, or thought I wanted him to. Geoffrey threw my bag into the trunk of the cab, and we left.

———————

At the ticket window, I hid Flash between my legs and the wall and told him it was serious so he needed to cooperate. We avoided waiting in the gate, making a beeline for the train door about five minutes before departure. Meeting with no resistance, Flash and I found our seats on the Northeast Regional bound for Penn Station. I studied his face. He stared at me adoringly. I was on a train with an animal, an animal I found on the street in a place where I didn't live, a street inhabited by many other good people who could have and probably would have taken him in had I only left him on the street. I knew this on Geoffrey's step, but I chose to transport Flash to New York City anyway, fully aware that Amtrak regulations prohibited his travel and that I lived in a Manhattan apartment building that banned pets. This was not romantic, rumbling over the Delaware River in such fashion. I hated Geoffrey P. Jamison. I was nuts about him. But I hated him.

———————

"I will be a few hours late," I told my mother from the pay phone on the platform in Princeton.

"Did you miss the one forty-five?"

"Just transferring."

"Why late then, mechanical trouble?"

The conductor had kicked us off the train. I thought that generic terms would be best.

"Dogs are not allowed on trains, so I had to get off in Princeton and wait. The next one's passing through in fifty minutes."

"What?"

"Fifty minutes, it's passing through in fifty minutes."

"What dogs?" my mother said.

"Well, a Yorkie, kind of." Flash pressed his head into my thigh.

The only breed of dog my mother recognized as such was the Yorkshire Terrier. All others were "beasts."

"Good god. Tell me you don't have an animal with you. Martin," she called to my father, "she has an animal with her."

She does.

"Bring a towel for the car, maybe. Beach size."

The conductors of the next two trains would not allow me to board. The conductor of the third reiterated the rules regarding all but seeing-eye dogs, but he said he'd bend them because his daughter was in veterinary school. He put me in the last car, which was closed off that day to other human beings, and animals, and climate control.

"Keep him away from the window, and when you get out, walk quickly, and talk to no one."

———

"What is it that you are lacking in your life, Samantha, that you needed to bring home a stray animal from Philadelphia?" my father asked after I secured my seat belt.

It was the nucleus of the issue, elucidated succinctly and precisely. I was sure that he knew what I was lacking, but he wanted me to state it, to hear the words bellow and hover, to expose me, embarrass me, teach me. My mother turned in her seat and cowered, as if she'd confronted a snow leopard. I looked out at Eighth Avenue, at people leaving their full-time non-month-to-month jobs, at couples in stride, at the beautiful day beyond the glass. I didn't answer my father's question.

Flash stepped all over my thighs and panted. He rubbed his nose on my neck and licked my chin. I didn't want him touching me or liking me or thinking that he was mine. I wanted to open the door and push him out, close my eyes while he fought me, shove him while he gripped me with his nails. Not look back as he found his way to the curb, tail tucked. I wanted to turn around, start over. Take me back to Our Lady. Forgive me Father, for I have sinned.

The next morning, my mother posted a sign at the school where she taught, and by three o'clock, Flash was excised from my life like the mushy part of a melon. A second-grade girl came with her parents to our front porch. She dropped to her knees and held his face, whispering that she couldn't believe it and that she loved him and would take care of him forever. I handed her Geoffrey's fashionable green leash, and she led Flash to their car.

"He's a nice dog," my mother called from the step, solidifying the arrangement. She stood for a brief moment and then hurried inside the house.

The little girl turned and waved. She bent down and hugged Flash with her entire body, flopping her chest onto his spine, her head onto his. She followed him into the rear seat, and they drove off.

Inside, my mother was starting dinner. "Well, that worked out. What a relief."

"Flash is a lucky boy."

"I'll say." She put a pan on the stove. "I thought I'd make the chicken you like, with the garlic. God knows how you managed for months without a kitchen."

I smiled. "Yeah, God knows."

CAUTION: MEN WORKING

They began yesterday at six fifty-nine a.m., one minute ahead of schedule. Twelve of them, in orange vests and droopy hats, tools in hand or under foot. They drove, whirling like dervishes in miniature tank vehicles, scraping and loading, lifting and lowering. They scooped. They ratcheted. They reminded me of something Balanchine would have choreographed, their display of coordination in the street mesmerizing, if not beautiful, on some level. But not my level. My level was desperate. Noisily desperate. Climb-into-the-dryer desperate.

For the entire day, the men bulldozed and jackhammered, producing sounds that I had never heard before, a snarly audio track of destruction too abrasive for a mammal such as myself, a mammal who was trying to complete mathematical calculations at a desk not twenty yards away. I computed two, maybe three, and then, realizing the futility, decided to clean out the kids' bathroom cabinets instead. For hours, I sorted ponytail accessories—elastics including the kind with the balls on the ends, stars on the ends, hearts on the ends—as well as barrettes, clips, bobbies, headbands and ribbons. I categorized contact solutions, dental flosses (is it *flossi?*), lotions—for itchy skin, sensitive skin, vanilla skin, strawberry skin—and the ever-critical battery of sunscreen products. I emerged lathered in cream, headbands on my head, cotton balls in my ears. By sundown, I had performed similar service on closets, baskets of magazines, the pantry and the aforementioned head, as my bangs needed trimming.

At six fifty-nine p.m., the racket ceased. In my door, a notice.

NOTICE, it said. Please remove your car from your driveway before seven a.m. tomorrow morning and do not return it to your driveway for three days, until after the cement we are pouring is cured. I needed curing. No, they needed curing. What was wrong with the street anyway?

I set my clock for six fifty-eight and when it rang, I went outside in my pajamas to find the men at the end of the driveway, waiting. Waiting for me. "There she is," one said beneath the clamor. It was loud, though I was certain that that is what he said. "Finally," said another.

Yeah, right. Out of my way, Mr. Bobcat.

I got into my car and drove it far, until I found a viable spot a half-mile away. I traipsed back, still in my pajamas, yes, mumbling like decompensated people do when they are outside in their pajamas. On the front steps of the house, I noticed in the window's reflection that my hair was sticking up like a carrot in one place on my crown and that another section was plastered sideways onto my cheek. It could have been worse, I thought. I checked to see that I was, in fact, wearing my pajamas. I looked down and saw that I was.

"Nice hair," one man said, beneath the clamor. It was loud, though I was certain that that is what he said.

I turned around and looked at him, and the rest of them in the road, leaning on their shovels, revving up the chopping machine, having laughs. I thought to blurt some made-up profanity and hurl it their way, but I went inside instead. Be the lady, my mother had said.

I would be more strategic on the second day of noise and take my mathematical calculations to a gentler environment, a library or coffee shop or interstate underpass. The first day, while sorting my daughters' ponytail holders, I pocketed several for myself. Paige and Emily wouldn't mind, if they could even tell, and I didn't take their favorites. Most important, I raised them to be good sharers, and they actually were. Sometimes, you grow people in your house, making it clear how you want them to act, but they resist. I stepped into the shower with a cap on my head, intending to lasso the mayhem on my scalp into one of their rubber bands with the hearts on the end, as it was not shampoo day. Shampoo day happened on Wednesdays.

I sudsed up my body from neck to toes and back up again, reserving the special face soap for my face, knowing that it was not special but enjoying the process that it imposed. I could hear the clatter of the jackhammer, even with water pounding into my ear canals.

Nice hair.

The remark returned to me while rubbing the special cleanser in a circular motion. Clockwise. Counter-clockwise. It's what it said to do.

Enough, I reached to turn off the faucet.

Outside, and in my shower, the chopping machine blurted, like gunfire. The bulldozer groaned.

I held the knob. No, not yet. I ripped off the plastic cap and stuck my head under the water shooting from on high, squirted shampoo straight from the bottle and worked it up into a bulging sphere. Standing in the tub, I pushed the curtain aside and found myself in the mirror across the room, glimpsing the froth that consumed my skull and face. With two hands, I patted the sides and heard the bubbles cave. *Shhhhh. Shhhh.* While rinsing, I decided that I wouldn't throw on shorts and a tee but would wear the nice jeans and the nice sandals with the heel, and the nice top. With the sash that tied in the back, or on the side, depending. Depending on your playfulness, your skepticism, your pluck.

I dried off, got dressed, blew out my nice hair. I applied eyeliner and mascara. Lipstick. Perfume. Yeah, perfume. I leaned up into the mirror in my sandals with the heels. Straightened out and checked the angles. Left. Right. Back.

At my desk, I gathered up my mathematical calculations and sketchbook and colored pencils and put them into my bag. The Bobcat twirled in the street, scraping and dumping, scraping and dumping. Drills cracked open the pavement. Men moved calmly in the racket like bugs on a hill, looked up when I left the house. Rested forearms on their shovels, dropped open their mouths, saying not a thing beneath the clamor. I was certain that that is what was said.

I slung my bag and descended the steps, strode out on the path and turned onto the sidewalk. The distance to the car was not long enough, it turned out. I took my time, heels clicking, sash swaying, locks lifting in a beautiful wind.

THE PROCLAMATION

Edward Strongmeyer wore oversized glasses, though his classmates wondered if he really needed them. His father was an optometrist, and the coincidence seemed too great. Edward looked like an optometrist himself.

Lizzie lived just around the corner from Ward Elementary, and her parents permitted her to walk home from school alone now that she was seven. Usually, she took the sidewalk that ringed the playground, but sometimes, she cut through the ballfield in the back of the building and crept under the metal fence. A former adventurer had scooped out a hole in the dirt directly under the chain link, prison-style, yielding a well-worn if not dirty egress from school property.

One afternoon, Edward appeared next to Lizzie on the pavement. She had no warning; he materialized like steam from a pothole. Often, she waited for her brother by the fourth-grade door and they'd walk home together, or sometimes, she and Linda Freedland would go together for part of the way, until Linda made the turn by the ranch house with the dentist's office inside. Linda was a capable kid with a generous and pleasing manner, and by all rights, the girls should have been terrific friends. But Mrs. Freedland yelled across the cul-de-sac to her sister-in-law, and Linda had a telephone in her room, both issues of concern to Lizzie, who questioned whether their sensibilities would mesh long-term. Their greatest commonality, she ultimately realized, was that neither of them took the bus.

Lizzie looked at Edward, wondering why he had chosen the

crew cut. At some point — in the car on the way to the barber, the moment the shaver is snatched from its hook — don't you catch yourself before the deed is done? Don't you scream out — Wait! — and bolt from the chair? Lizzie moved away from Edward, toward the strip of grass that flanked the curb.

He coughed, dredging phlegm from his throat. Then he told Lizzie that he loved her, just like that. "I love you, Lizzie."

The words spewed from his mouth, elongated and bellowing, landing on Lizzie like a virus. She couldn't say the things that sprang into her brain. How dare you, or Go away, or You have big gums and Don't you know you've just ruined everything? In that instant, she was forced to engage with a boy, handle his feelings, ascertain hers and worse, present them in a statement in front of the Florentinos' split-level. She could have pretended a mountain lion was behind them, and run. She could have run anyway, without the lion. She could have grabbed Jennifer Simpson, seven steps ahead, and asked her what kind of cover she was making for the book report.

But she continued to walk, switching her lunchbox to her right hand, creating a physical barrier. She now hugged the curb, despite her parents' warnings about getting too close to the road. Edward kept pace, silently, having spoken his piece. Lizzie quickened her steps. Her stomach shot into her throat. She pulled up her hood.

Lizzie believed that Edward could not possibly love her. She had given him no opportunity. She turned and looked at his face. The sun hit his lenses, rendering them white, like blazing snowballs, and obstructing her view of his eyes. Lizzie hated Edward in that moment. She didn't despise him before the proclamation; she didn't even notice him. Wouldn't he rather have been ignored than detested? It was nonsensical as well as presumptuous. How brazen of Edward Strongmayer to disrupt her calm, to intrude upon her tranquility, on the sidewalk and into her very core.

Cowardly, or ineptly or pre-pubescently, but probably cowardly, Lizzie chose to say nothing. "I will say nothing," she said in her head. There. How about that. "I will proceed down the path as I do every afternoon, thinking about the day, about what I will do next. This boy will not disturb my after-school routine or the way I want to do it. He will not make me respond. He will not make me not be me."

So, Lizzie tried to carry on as if it were Before Edward and made her way down the little hill, around the bend by the Buddha statue, onto the straightaway and into home. But, despite her determination, there was still a body next to her, matching her stride in a swishy parka. Edward had succeeded to occupy space and mind that had been Lizzie's alone. Not only was he intruding onto her pavement, he had gotten her to think about something she never thought about in her entire childhood. Him.

He shuffled alongside her down Bayberry Way to her front door, where he stood, like a rash. She didn't know what he expected her to do. He could not have believed that she would have loved him back, or even said the words, just because he did. But he waited on the slate steps, under the sea anemone light fixture, for something. Lizzie rang the bell. And rang again, pressing hard and fast. Edward coughed mucus into his mouth and muttered, a string of sputum stretching from his top lip to the bottom. He rubbed his hand over the prickles on his head, and Lizzie sensed another utterance, knowing that this time, she'd be reeled in, sucked into his delusion and gall, the last place she wanted to go. She leaped over the pachysandra and tore into the open garage, careening onto the button that operated the electric door. As it descended, she spun around and saw the two white orbs, struck again by the sun, and then the remainder of Edward planted firmly on the gravel, erased from sight inch by inch, to nothing.

She ran up to her lavender room and hid until he had gone. The notion that a boy could love her was humiliating. It felt as if something was being taken away, not bestowed.

Her bedroom was situated in the front of the house. Two of the windows faced the street. She crouched below the sill, her knees jammed into her ribs. If she rose carefully, to her bottom lashes, she could peer down to the right and see the driveway. Uneasy about leaving Edward's whereabouts in a questionable state, Lizzie needed to see that he had actually retreated. Slowly, she unbent her legs and stretched upwards, her cheek gliding along the textured wallpaper. Mrs. Sondra Wheeler, the home's former inhabitant, had installed a bristly wall covering years earlier, rendering a hieroglyphic effect. Lizzie's mother painted over it in the lavender, Lizzie's choice. Sondra's decorating skill was generally revered, and much of what she had chosen remained in the house, in some form.

"This tub is the ultimate," Lizzie's mom, Bev, had said of the sunken blue porcelain. "And the bidet, incredible."

Incredible, maybe, though Lizzie presumed through adolescence that it was a foot bath and was permitted to use it as such.

Her face exfoliated, she reached the sill. Edward was where she had left him, looking bewildered in the middle of the driveway. From higher up, he appeared less disgusting to Lizzie, though she knew better. Edward tilted his head back, and Lizzie ducked down in a jolt. She pressed her ear into the wall and could feel every tremor, every shift of terrain. She could hear all infinitesimal sounds, magnified and foreboding. A crow crowed. It could have been a pterodactyl. At precisely three thirty-five p.m. on her red Timex, the Earth rumbled, vibrating her cranium on Sondra Wheeler's wall covering. She gripped the dresser leg next to her and curled up like a fiddlehead fern, uncertain of the tumult's origin but thinking that somehow, whatever it was, it was her fault. She had been callous and now, some kind of cosmic unrest had been unleashed upon Bayberry Way. Or, Mr. Strongmayer had sensed emotional upheaval in his young son's life and had landed on the driveway in his mobile eyeglass unit, covered with "E" charts and outfitted with vats of that solution that bends your frames. Summoning strength, Lizzie rose to face the destiny beyond her bedroom window. It was Bev Michaelson, in the Chevy Monza.

Edward had vanished. A puff of exhaust hovered over the spot. Lizzie slunk down to the floor and leaned against the wall, her spine quivering with the descent of the electric door.

Home early from work, her mother headed up the second bank of stairs and into the room, where Lizzie remained balled up on the floor, her fuschia snow coat bunching into her neck. Her hair shot out from the static and clung to the hieroglyphics behind her, suctioning her in place. She heard the swish of lining from her mother's skirt before it appeared in the doorway.

"Take off your coat, sweetie."

Lizzie didn't move.

Mrs. Michaelson raised the window shade to half-mast. "Are you feeling sick?"

Lizzie shook her head.

Mrs. Michaelson crouched down and felt Lizzie's cheek. "Then what are you doing crumpled up on the floor?"

"I don't know."

"Get up then, and come have a snack."

"There's a crack over my closet, you know."

"Oh, that line? It's nothing, just from the settling. But don't tell your father, or he'll have the men in here."

"What men?"

"The ceiling men. They make such a mess."

"Are there different men for different things?"

"There are all kinds."

"Like floor men?"

"Sure, there are floor men. We had them in your room, remember?"

Lizzie became lightheaded, and her toes felt numb.

"I'm going to get out of this skirt," Mrs. Michaelson said, kissing Lizzie on her electrified head.

———————

The next day in school, Edward appeared in places where he hadn't before, and he stared at Lizzie as if he had newfound permission. He allowed himself to gawk and ogle, now, after having allowed himself to stalk her on the sidewalk in a neighborhood where he didn't even live. He sat at the end of Lizzie's lunch table, leering over a bologna sandwich. He turned up on the swing next to hers at recess, mimicking the sweep of her legs, kicking in tandem. Lizzie squirmed and grew queasy. She groaned and flew off the swing. She ran from Edward, but she didn't challenge him, and he derived encouragement, or entitlement, from the response or lack thereof.

Their class went to the library in the afternoon. The kids formed a circle on the carpet, leaving a space for the librarian's chair as they did each Wednesday. Edward hovered, waiting to sit down. Lizzie chose a strategic position next to Linda Freed-land on one side and the empty spot on the other, secure in the belief that no one would trespass on Mrs. Noble's turf, not even Edward. Lizzie put her hand into the space, a placeholder, and watched for Mrs. Noble over her shoulder, bouncing her criss-crossed knees. On typical Wednesdays, Mrs. Noble wheeled her chair to the circle in a flurry of enthusiasm, two books in hand, glasses on her head, right on time. She read like an actress, weep-ing or whispering or speaking in brogue, accenting her words with grimaces, grins and the flying of arms. Whoever was in the library stopped what they were doing to listen and watch. Edward wouldn't dare steal her seat.

Lizzie saw Mrs. Noble across the room at her desk, gathering up the books and corralling the back of her chair. Simultaneously, Edward took a step toward her spot, and another one. Their classroom teacher, Mrs. Reed, approached him, extending her arm toward the floor where they stood while two kids below them made room. Not interested, Edward continued around the back of the circle, heading where no student had gone before, defying order and expectation to satisfy himself. Lizzie jogged her head from Mrs. Noble to Edward, and Edward to Mrs. Noble, her heart rate spiking as they converged on the vacancy next to her. Flush and sweaty, she hit the floor with her palm and pleaded with Mrs. Noble to move more quickly, to get there already, to save her, her whispers becoming calls, becoming outright yells.

"Hurry, Mrs. Noble, you have to hurry," Lizzie screamed, pierc-ing the library's quiet. Heads turned from all over the room. "And you, get away from me and stay away for the rest of your life."

Her classmates were still, mouths agape. Mrs. Noble let go of her chair and knelt down next to Lizzie, who convulsed with sobs, her face in her hands. Edward took another step, but Mrs. Reed pulled him back. Mrs. Noble helped Lizzie stand up and led her out of the library and down the hall.

"He followed me to my house. And said things."

"I'm so sorry, dear," Mrs. Noble said, reciting the words with compassion, crinkling her eyes. "Nurse Patty can help."

Lizzie wiped her face and dropped her hand from Mrs. Noble's. "I'm not sick. He said things."

Mrs. Noble opened the door to the nurse's office, motioning with her eyes for assistance. She deposited Lizzie and left.

In the library, Edward had broken free from Mrs. Reed and proceeded to Lizzie's spot in the circle, where he sat, his chin lifted and arms folded neatly across his stomach. Mrs. Noble picked up the first book, pulled her glasses onto her nose and read.

AS CRIMINALS GO

L ight entered the newsroom through foot-wide strips of window, and at a certain point in the late afternoon, fantastic ribbons of dust shot out from the walls like laser beams. When this happened, the education reporter complained of the glare and got up and resituated herself at the assignment desk. She fancied herself some sort of starlet, wearing red lipstick and velvet chokers around her neck, a different color each day. Her big story was about air conditioning; there was none in the county's elementary schools, and the children were melting onto the floor way before they could think about long division. Mississippi had heat that could make you forget your name. The ribbon around the education reporter's neck must have felt like a vise. It gave the impression that it performed some function, like seam binding or mailing tape.

Early in my tenure, the news director walked into the room one morning and tapped his fingers on my desk. "Venuzzi's being arraigned today. You ready?"

I jumped up. This was a huge criminal case. I had been covering zoning board meetings and fishing contests that were called rodeos, as if the mackerel and spadefish bucked and jumped fences. People brought their catch in coolers and held each fish by the gills for measuring. They stuck their chests out and smiled for photos.

"They've got him on racketeering and murder," John said. "County Court. Ten a.m. Make sure you follow him from the car on up the steps and get plenty of close-ups. I want tight shots of his filthy face, you hear?"

"Got it." I threw extra reporter pads and pens into my bag.

"He won't talk to you going in, but see what you can do on the way out, unless they take him through the back."

"We'll go around the back, then."

John laughed. "You get through, and you're the news director."

P.J. Venuzzi was known in the region as the don of the Dixie Mafia. He had smuggled more than his share of illegal drugs through the Gulf of Mexico into ports in Alabama, Mississippi and Louisiana. Though no one had been able to catch him, it was understood that he had killed a fine collection of Southern men in the name of business.

"Do they really have him on murder?" I asked.

"Looks like. Now go. Benny's shooting."

"And Sam," he said as we began for the door, "watch out. This guy's a real sweet talker."

I hadn't thought of Mr. Venuzzi as a man in a position to flirt.

Benny grabbed our gear, and we headed out.

"You're in a hurry this mornin'," the education reporter said as we passed her desk. She was talking to Benny. "Anywhere good?"

"A little something at the courthouse."

"With her?"

It was already 102 degrees in the parking lot. My northern thermostat was going haywire. Her choker was violet.

Benny loaded up the van. "You sure do get under Kelly Sue's skin. Must be some kind of new-girl rivalry going on there."

"C'mon, women in the south aren't competitive, you know that."

We pulled out of the lot and drove west along the beach road toward Gulfport, the county seat. I prepared questions, and Benny went over the basics for maneuvering in a group. I hadn't been in the position to vie for an interview when a story was breaking, and this one would have a crowd.

Gulfport was a sleepy place, until you hit the courthouse. There, the town jumped alive, seersucker vents flapping up and down the steps like turbines. Justice in motion. I imagined the crime as it happened, the deserted lot, the ditch beside the road. But to see the man, days later, showered, calm...wasn't there time, a beat, to grab oneself by the neck and stop? Did he consider his conscience and proceed anyway? Was there no conscience? The question of questions.

Venuzzi was to arrive in the sheriff's car at the front of the courthouse and proceed up the main steps. Crews from stations all over the state, as well as Louisiana and Alabama, had arrived earlier in the morning. I would have to beat out the other reporters, all from larger markets, to get a comment. I wanted something, it didn't matter what. I just wanted mine to be the one question he stopped for and answered.

Right at ten, the deputy drove up, followed by several police units. They took their marks around the car carrying Venuzzi and let him out. He was cuffed at the wrists, wearing the short-sleeved orange jumpsuit of the Harrison County Correction Department, HCCD stenciled in black across his scapulas.

The officers guided him down the walk as my fellow journalists hurled questions in his direction. John did say that it was unusual for a suspect to comment before a proceeding and that the policemen would want to get him inside as fast as possible. But I sensed that this new occupation of mine was not entirely predictable. Certainly, there were procedures, legal and ethical ones that were binding, but out on the street, it was all feel.

The other reporters continued to call out questions, all of which went unheeded. They moved laterally, keeping a distance, in a pack. They yelled at once. Their words were the same, sentences the same, starting and stopping in unison. I motioned to Benny to slow down, and I hung back, inserting space between us and the crowd and moving forward, toward our subject, changing directions. My voice would come from a different angle, by itself. It would ping through the air and into his ear and make him turn. But I'd have to be fast, before his escorts realized and pushed us back.

"Mr. Venuzzi," I called, just a few feet behind him. He took another step, almost to the door, and stopped, swiveling. I took a deep breath and stretched out my mic. "Mr. Venuzzi, did you take a gun and put it in your hand and shoot Mr. Albanese in the spine six times while he was eating lasagna?" A lull. "With spinach?"

The pack, yards away, stopped moving and became quiet. Benny crept up closer behind my shoulder.

Venuzzi lowered his chin and peered over his sunglasses. "Miss

Kent," he said. The other reporters ruffled their notebooks and snapped their heads. "Welcome to Mississippi."

I waited a beat, keeping him engaged, giving Benny time to zoom in. Sweating. "Thank you," I said to the cordial murderer who somehow knew my name and the length of my residence in the state. "I'm happy to be here."

Venuzzi set his head straight and walked inside the building. When the door shut, I spun around toward Benny.

"Ooh-wee, creepy, *Miss Kent*," he said, turning off the camera, "but good."

"Really?"

"Let's just say John'll be running promos of that 'til the next millennium."

During the year that I worked in Biloxi, I was given many exclusive interviews with Venuzzi, in prison rooms, at police headquarters, in lawyers' offices when he was out on bail. At every proceeding we covered, every walk to the court or ride to the jail, he raised his cuffed hands and waved to me. And only me.

"Good morning, Miss Kent."

"Nice day today, Miss Kent."

I'd nod my head, acknowledging the greeting, feeling the other reporters' eyes on me. At first, they teased me, called me the Mob Mistress, and I laughed about it, too, because it certainly was something to be teased about. But then, the tone changed. They stopped saying hello out in the field, on other stories where we'd all be. Once, I overheard two of them talking at a press conference. "Kind of whorish," said one; "...if she was any good at her job…" said the other.

The don of the Dixie Mafia was fond of me, yes. Or he liked luring me, maybe. I did nothing to encourage the attention, and I wasn't going to apologize for it or be naive about it, either. The offensive part was not that it was sexual, or even untoward. I had been noticed by men who shouldn't have noticed. Professors, supervisors at summer jobs. Unlike those guys, Venuzzi was never inappropriate—in fact, he was overly polite—and, of course, I was never alone with him. He couldn't act upon his impulses, if he had them, which he knew, and I knew. Less could be said for the others.

What felt unsettling was the idea that the same person who

killed people also enjoyed interacting with me, looking at me. But I couldn't tell him not to look at a person who was talking with him, or tell him to look only a certain way. So, he looked, and I tried to steer him where I led, hoping that he'd tell me what he'd tell no one else. The journalistic jackpot. I asked the questions, and he looked. I pried, and he looked. And the lawyers sat in the room and watched it. They watched me talk. They watched me take off a sweater, put on a sweater, cross a leg, turn in my chair, thinking that every motion was an enticement. *That* was violating.

"So, what's it like?" I asked him during one of our interviews.

"Prison? They're pretty nice to me."

"No, doing bad things. What's it like doing bad things?"

He lifted his hands from his lap and set them on the table. The cuffs clunked. "You could ask anybody that question, and I reckon someone could ask you."

He stared at me, his green eyes fixed on mine. I felt Benny narrow the camera lens behind my back. I felt myself swallow and say nothing.

One lawyer leaned against the wall behind Venuzzi, shirted arms crossed. He smirked and kicked up his chin. His partner stared right at me, dropping his gaze to my chest, skirt, legs.

I pulled my notebook onto my lap and straightened in the chair. Don't answer the interviewee, I told myself. You ask the questions. You create the discomfort. You maneuver him.

I looked down at my pad, scribbled nonsense on it for show. Made a serious thinking expression, nodded as if the ideas were forming when they weren't. I hadn't provoked this, I told myself. I just crossed one leg over the other, got warm and took off a sweater. Took off a sweater as anyone would in a hot room in a Mississippi jail. But it felt indecent, all of a sudden. I felt indecent. I felt tawdry. Responsible. Dumb.

The men waited for me to speak. I flipped a page in my notepad, scanning the thoughts I had prepared in the van. A blur.

Benny bent, pretending to adjust the foot of the tripod. "Ask it again," he whispered.

I looked up and took a breath. "So," I started and stopped. "So, Mr. Venuzzi, when you do the bad things, do you feel a certain way afterward?"

He laughed. Skin crinkled around his eyes. "C'mon, Miss Kent, you're better than that. What do you think?"

I waited.

He leaned forward. The cuffs slid toward me. "Well, you think something, don't you?"

"I think, Mr. Venuzzi, that you're saying you do bad things."

One lawyer looked at the other. The guard by the door shot me a glance. Venuzzi soured.

"Is that what you're saying?" I asked, tilting my chin, letting my hair fall out from behind my ear. "Are you a bad man, Mr. Venuzzi?"

He winced. His skin flushed. The tape ran.

"I think we've got what we need," I told Benny, my eyes trained across the table.

The guard approached Venuzzi and lifted him up by the arm. He shuffled out, his ankles clanking like rocks down a cliff.

THE INTERLOPER

One Saturday night, Nancy Norton arrived at our house with chocolate fudge and a box of pound cake, each slice wrapped and sealed in factory cellophane. Three of the twelve original portions were missing, giving the remaining dessert items ample room in which to flop and crinkle as she walked.

"Just take the pound cake," Nancy's mother must have said. "We only ate a few of them."

Matt let Nancy into the house while I watched TV in the den. "Ooh, what's in the bag?" he asked, squeezing the contents. He looked inside. "Mmm, pound cake."

"You hate pound cake," I said to myself.

"And hot fudge, too," Nancy added. "We can put it on top, with ice cream."

"Oh, hi," I said, sauntering into the foyer.

"Oh, hi," she said, tying up the bag.

"Did you bring ice cream?" Matt asked.

Having a first girlfriend must be hard enough to navigate, without a younger sister hovering around. But it was, after all, Saturday night, my favorite evening of the week, and this time, it was my brother's turn to keep me company. My father didn't like the idea of leaving me home by myself, thinking I'd wallow in my fourteen-year-old solitude when really, I rather enjoyed the peace. So, he would break movie dates with Mom, despite her entreaties and mine, choosing instead to eat pistachios and play Monopoly with me on the stone table that chimed with the sound of the dice. On this particular night, my father's office was having its annual fete, so he asked Matt to stay home. If Nancy wanted to see her boyfriend, she would have to endure her boyfriend's sister, me, his biggest fan.

My parents instructed us to root for each other and protect each other, though they didn't really need to tell me to do that, and I can only hope that they didn't need to tell Matt, either. Parents say certain important things just to know that kids have heard them. Take care of your sister. Keep the hair dryer off the sink. If we hear these statements a second time, or a sixth, that is fine. It's fine to tell us again about the hair dryer. We get it, after a certain age. We know that it makes them feel better or think they've warded it off, just saying that we could get electrocuted, or run over, or swept up by a tidal wave.

I didn't like Nancy Norton, and not only because she was a pushy and self-centered sixteen-year-old, or because she had the platform wedgie shoes that my parents prohibited me from wearing. She was easily agitated, about insignificant things. She squealed when a giggle was enough. She cried when a math test was hard. In our house, dwelling on nonsense wasn't tolerated. For a short period in first grade, I couldn't pick out which clothes to put on, falling down naked on my bed every morning, exasperated. After a week of this, my father came into my room with five small squares of paper, onto which he had written the names of the school days, Monday through Friday. Without saying anything, he opened my closet, retrieved one dress at a time and pierced its hanger through the homemade tags. In a swoop, he pushed the remaining garments off to one side of the rack, out of contention. Then, he left. The next Monday, I woke up, ate a Pop Tart and put on the designated dress.

There was trouble bubbling beneath Nancy Norton's overreactions and trendy clothing, defective thoughts and plans stirring about. She was in for a tumultuous ride, and under no circumstance was it to take place in my brother's Buick Skylark. I would have to snatch command of the future, called as if from the deities themselves to step up and intervene.

"Is it raining?" I asked her. "Your hair is like a ten on the Frizz-o-meter."

She whipped her head around into the foyer mirror. "It is not.

It's straight, like it always is."

Matt watched Nancy flatten her hair into her ear lobes.

She turned toward him, elbows jutting. "It's not frizzy, is it?"

"A little bit, but it doesn't look bad or anything."

I went into the living room and sat down at the piano. Something somber, perhaps. Foreboding. "The Mozart," I whispered. "Fantasia in D minor. Perfect."

During the long rests in the composition, I eavesdropped. It was as much my duty to observe this relationship as it was my brother's to babysit me. Dad would get double coverage, and I was happy to serve. A full report would be presented the following morning.

Matt and Nancy headed for the kitchen. Time for cake. The Fantasia ended with four giant chords, double forte. I turned off the sconce behind me and followed.

Nancy stood by the island, clasping her fingers over the jar of fudge, twisting the lid. Her upper arms spread out and flanked her body like ears on a Bassett hound.

"What do you do if you can't reach the octaves?" Matt asked. "I mean, say you're a great pianist, but you just don't have the anatomy."

"I think the best pianists, the concert pianists, have the fingers. It may not be fair, but it could be the thing that makes them the best."

Nancy continued to struggle with the cap. Her lips puckered. Her torso folded onto itself. She turned pink.

"You can't be a high jumper if your legs are short," I went on. "It's just the wrong shape."

Grunts came from behind the island. Matt and I sat at the table and couldn't see Nancy, as she had fallen below counter level in her effort to remove the lid.

Matt leaned back and crossed a leg. "I guess that makes sense. Natural selection. The best swimmers have long arms."

"Like wings." I heard a gasp. "I think she may need help."

Matt got up and peered over the island and down at the floor. "What is this for again?"

"You heat it up and pour it on top of the ice cream," said Nancy, squinting into the overhead light.

"I thought you brought cake or something."

"I did. I told you, you put this on it. You melt it, and you put it on top. I told you in the foyer."

I slid my stomach onto the counter. Nancy had clearly planned a cake itinerary for the evening. I will not do that when I am sixteen.

Winded, she scowled up at us, the jar in her lap. "Don't you have homework or something, or a little friend you could call?"

"And miss this? No thank you."

She rose to her full height, blew air out of her mouth and stomped her wedgie. Matt took the jar from her hand and opened it. Nancy snatched it back and placed it into a saucepan filled with water and heated it on the stove. When the chocolate was hot, she went into our cabinet and took out two of our plates, onto which she piled the toasted cake, scoop of ice cream and warmed-up fudge. She set our dishes on our table, with our two forks and two napkins. Matt followed her and sat back down, across from me. She looked exhausted.

"Oh, you didn't want any, did you?" she asked me, removing our fork from her mouth.

"Have some. It's pretty good," Matt said.

I did not want her insipid prefabricated cake tower. I did not want to laud her audacious girlfriend behavior. I wanted to eradicate her, but first, I wanted to toy with her fragile self-esteem.

"I don't eat pound cake."

"I didn't think so."

"Unless it's the bakery kind."

———

My mother suggested to Matt that he caddy at a local golf club to earn money for the high school prom. The explicit message that he would have to lug iron clubs on his back in order to buy tickets, dinner and a wrist corsage for Nancy Norton struck me as a brilliant parental strategy. It incorporated so many lessons, and the big ones, too—hard work, self-sufficiency, consequences, planning—while also intimating that no assistance would be provided given that Nancy Norton was the date in question. Following the cake tower debriefing the morning after, I got the feeling that my parents thought less of her presence in my brother's life than they had previously.

"I think the caddying is fantastic," I complimented them one night during dinner. "There are no carts, right?"

Matt looked up from his plate. "No carts?"

"Gee, I don't know," said Mom. "You think there are carts, Bill?"

"Oh, I have no idea," my father said. "Walking is better exercise, anyway."

Before going to sleep that night, I asked my dad whether they would have required the job had Matt chosen a different date.

"Of course. And Nancy's a nice girl."

"What?"

"Oh, she's not so bad," said my wise and scholarly father, my insanely smart and analytical role model, turning in his flannel slipper and proceeding down the hallway.

How could she be mean to me and a nice girl all at once? Certainly, he couldn't have thought that I was just a bothersome little sister or Nancy Norton a mere victim of puppy love. What was he saying, really. There must have been an underlying meaning that I was supposed to excavate, like a ruby in a batch of marbles. Did Mom know about this? Why couldn't they just hate her and tell her to go away?

———————

Upon returning from his first morning of caddying, Matt pulled open his shirt and showed us his shoulder. The expanse of skin over the collarbone was chafed red and lined with multiple vertical impressions. In places, it appeared that the dermis had been cut away, curled at the edges like roll-up shades. The wound would need antibiotic ointment and bandaging. It would sting in the shower. By the following Saturday, my mother had implanted a sanitary pad into the underside of my brother's shirt, sewing it into the fabric with thread. Without hesitation, Matt proceeded to the golf course healed and buffeted, his caddying shoulder ready for action, and whatever else.

———————

Two months after the prom, my parents and I drove Matt to Boston for college. We set up his room, made his bed and unpacked his clothing. After a walk through the campus green, we got into the car and headed home. I put my legs up on the back seat, newly vacant, but that felt weird so I put them in front of me, where they normally went.

————————

My parents didn't mention Nancy once Matt left for school. I realized then that they believed the high school romance would fade naturally, which must have accounted for my father's casual reaction to Nancy's distasteful behavior in the spring. Since Matt never talked about her while away at college, we presumed the relationship had ended as expected.

But by October, junior-girl talk had gossiped down to the sophomores, and I caught wind that Nancy was still Matt's girl-friend, or she believed that she was. The revelation sent my primi-tive reflexes into protection mode, heightening my powers of smell, hearing and sight and catapulting them squarely into the cabinet to the right of Matt's bed.

Magnetically, my hands latched onto the knob and pulled open the door. Once inside, they transcended a pile of used notebooks and flew to the space beyond, where they confronted two stacks of envelopes, business size, bound in rubber bands. I floated the stash over the books, careful not to disrupt the scene, and extri-cated them from their foxhole into the light of truth, if not my brother's sailboat-papered room with the gingham trim.

Inside each envelope was a letter. Eighty-seven in all, a body of work. One each day from the moment he matriculated until Thanksgiving, when he brought them home. There really was no quandary for me about whether to read them; the question was whether to involve Mom, who could prohibit me from opening them, thereby setting me up to disobey, which was something I did not relish doing or accomplish particularly well when I did.

I decided to begin unaided and see where the road would weave.

"I am half a human with you gone."

"No, less than half."

Gasp.

"I can hardly breathe until we are married and sharing an office."

"My world is black."

"Mom!" I called to my mom, shaking the letters over the banister like maracas.

"What are those?" she asked, coming through the kitchen door.

I handed her a long one, written on yellow paper. She read both sides, still grasping a ladle. "Are those the same?"

I nodded.

"I need you to love me forever, until we die," Mom read out loud.

"That's after they share office space, when they're attorneys." I handed her another.

"I thought he wanted to be a vet."

I laid out the letters on the dining room table, and Mom stood silently in front of them. Her eyes jumped from one envelope to the next, like a CIA agent before a wall of clues. We opened each letter and placed its envelope on top, knowing we would have to return them to the cabinet as they had been found.

"This can't go on, obviously," I said.

"Obviously."

———

Three weeks later, my mom and I picked Matt up at the train station when he came home from college for Christmas. When we saw him step onto the platform, we got out of the car and waved like banshees, probably not the only people to do so along the northeast corridor that day. We kissed him on dueling cheeks, linked his arms and led him to the parking spot.

Mom's plan was to dispose of Nancy as early in the week as possible. She waited for an opening. On the way home, Matt mentioned that Nancy wanted to come to the house and see him that afternoon. He hadn't seen her since he left for school in August. He did not appear enthusiastic.

"Do you want to see her?" Mom asked.

"Yeah."

"Are you sure?"

"Yeah."

"But not really?"

"Not really."

Mom was good.

"Maybe you'd like to date other girls at school?"

He nodded.

Really good.

"Take her for a walk," she said.

"Today?"

"Today."

I had offered to sequester myself somewhere where I could keep an eye, but Mom banished me to the backyard instead. Feeling instrumental and rather catalytic, really, in the ultimate riddance of Nancy Norton, I was not content to romp among the dormant zucchini plants, missing the resolution that I had anticipated for so long.

Finding a loose-fitting screen in the powder room window, I forced up the glass with my fingertips, creating a hairline latitudinal crack. It was, for God's sakes, the era of Woodward and Bernstein. I believed that Nancy would resist. She would not acquiesce and leave; she would threaten my brother with her physical and psychological well-being. She would say her heart will pump no more.

Mom instructed Matt to have Nancy come at five, so that dinnertime would provide a fixed end to the conversation.

"Walk to the corner, then around the block the short way. If you are not finished by five-thirty, I will come outside and call to you, so listen for me and be ready," she said. "I'll say it's the phone."

I wanted to do that part.

After reading the letters, I was angry that my brother had to fend off the responsibility that Nancy imposed upon him. He needed to cut her off, snip the line and let her drop. It also occurred to me that he may have brought the letters home so that they would be found. First girlfriends could be hard to dump all by yourself. He went outside before Nancy had the chance to ring the bell.

"Remember, focus on you, say that *you* can't do it," Mom prepped him at the door.

"Okay, I've got it."

"Say nothing negative about her, understand?"

I came out of the powder room into the foyer.

"He went," Mom said.

"I know."

"How long have you been in there?"

"Long enough. Those jeans look terrible on her."

I followed Mom into the kitchen and helped her make a salad. She had no patience for chopping. Never sharpened a knife.

The phone rang.

"Just went outside," Mom said.

"Is that Dad?" I whispered.

Mom blinked yes.

A combined effort, fantastic. Dad remained in the background, as it was an issue that involved teen romance, but he was privy and in constant contact. An advisory role.

"Five-thirty," she said. "Pork chops."

"And salad," I added.

"And salad."

Mom retrieved four sweet potatoes from their cool dark place, scrubbed the skin and put them in the oven. I sprinkled raisins, smashed pretzels and Rice Krispies on the salad.

"I'm going to go check," I said.

"Do we need the Rice Krispies?"

It was five-twenty. From the bathroom window, I had a clear view of the driveway and part of the street. I stood with my back and left cheekbone flat against the wall, the way policemen do to ambush a heroin house. I could not see anyone out of my left eye but slunk down anyway and crawled out of the room.

Mom stood at the threshold. "Anything?"

"I don't see them yet."

At five twenty-five, Mom stepped out onto the porch. We could hear yelling, and more yelling. Mom couldn't wait.

"Yoohoo, Matt," she called. "Yoohoo."

Nancy was screeching, and it was hard to hear what she was saying, exactly, but the tone was entirely discernible. Mom hurried to the end of the driveway and waved her arms overhead.

"Telephone," she called. "It's for you, come quickly."

Matt saw her and started for the house. Nancy continued to

scream at him. He ignored her and picked up the pace.

Mom grasped his elbow. "Get inside, fast."

"Wow," he said, stumbling through the screen.

"She'll just go home."

"I'll watch," I said.

"You will not," Mom said.

"What did she say? She sounded nuts."

"It doesn't matter," Mom said. "That's it. Done."

She put the pork chops under the broiler just as Dad came through the garage. He set down his attaché case and embraced Matt with both arms. "There's the college boy. Let's take a look at you."

He held onto Matt's back and kissed me on the forehead. "What do you think of your big brother? Six months. Tremendous."

I waited for some acknowledgment of what had just happened. A question about how he felt, a word of consolation, a reminder of all the better girls waiting for him on the other side. Something.

But Dad said nothing about Nancy, like an assassin after a rub-out. Matt and Mom joined in the silence, job completed.

"How soon do we eat? Missed lunch today," Dad said, washing his hands. "And what an interesting salad," he smiled, looking over his shoulder to the counter.

At dinner, while everyone talked about Matt's classes and activities and roommates, I wondered if Nancy had made it home or instead, driven to the pier to wade out into the Hudson, over the rocks at the edge to its center, where the currents would sweep her south. My brother wasn't wondering; if anything, he looked relieved. Mom wasn't wondering, either. I put my bet on Dad, the just man, weigher of good and evil. But he'd do it later, when he didn't have to look as if he wasn't. Task at hand, he liked to say.

Clearly, I, too, was thrilled that Nancy Norton was gone, but I felt bad for her at that moment, my belly full of pork chops, the table set for the four of us, again. She had been tossed aside, and that can't have felt good, even if it was better for her, and Matt, in the end. But we weren't thinking about what was better for her. Protection didn't extend beyond the bonds of family, beyond blood.

Maybe I felt compassion for her because I no longer felt threatened. That is no way to feel compassion.

WORD GAME

The Sylvania arrived in 1970, crossing the threshold of our suburban Colonial like jetsam from a futuristic ship. We were part of Progress. We had a color TV.

Until then, we were happy enough with the black and white Zenith in the corner of our parents' bedroom, even if we had to nudge the antennas to clear out the picture. We sat on the floor, close by, scooting across the carpet when the screen fuzzed. Dad said that we needed to back up, at least to the foot of the bed. Our eyes would scramble if we didn't, and of course there was the radiation.

When the Sylvania came, the Zenith went to the spare room downstairs, where Mary Jane lived, the second housekeeper to inhabit the space. Betty was the first, hired two weeks before my mother took a retail job in White Plains. One of Betty's hands was missing fingers, but she could tie shoelaces and attach safety pins and chop whatever needed chopping for dinner. Betty lived in our finished basement from Sunday evening until the following Friday, when she left to go home. Two decades of African American women followed her, making the weekly trip from a New York borough to Westchester County, by taxi, train and bus, earning money to send to family. Sons, daughters, husbands, nieces…we never quite knew.

Mary Jane worked in a beer factory in Milwaukee before moving to New York to clean homes. She was in her twenties, slim and efficient. She zipped through our split-level, climbing on step stools and squeezing behind bureaus, her baby blue uniform a streak of fluidity and flair. Our house was never so pristine. After school, Mary Jane and I played games in a spiral notebook, word hunts, mainly, in ballpoint pen. She was smart, and even as a kid, I sensed that her work for us might have been temporary, that she had other plans. The spare room was large enough for a twin bed and bureau. The Zenith perched on a gold metal stand that had wheels and a basket underneath. Sometimes, the set was tuned to a soap opera when we hunted for the words.

One afternoon soon after the Sylvania was situated upstairs, Mary Jane taped a square sheet of pliable plastic to the front of her new TV. It was striped in a rainbow of colors. The black and white images behind it turned yellow or turquoise or red, without regard for what they were and what color they should have been. A person's face was half-purple, half-blue. An apple, orange. An orange, green. The plastic had been folded, and it bulged in the middle. Mary Jane pressed it into the screen and secured extra tape above the crease and below.

"*Transportation*," she said, adjusting the angle of the stand. "Write that one down."

I opened the notebook to a clean page and spelled the word out in all capitals. She sat on the bed and did the same on a sheet of paper, propped on her knee. I handed her the TV Guide to put underneath for support.

"No apostrophes, right?" I asked.

"Nope. That makes it too easy."

From the TV, a laundry detergent jingle sang out. The arms of a woman folding clothes were hot pink. Her legs were aqua. Mary Jane looked up when the soap opera resumed.

She wagged her finger at a man in the scene, a man whose skin was chartreuse. "Ooh, he's in trouble." Mary Jane said nothing of the uncoordinated colors.

I remembered the man from a previous time we played the word game, though I didn't follow the plot of the show. I wasn't allowed to watch TV after school, so I felt sort of disobedient and tried not to look. My parents gave Mary Jane clothes to take with her on Fridays, on the Fridays that she left, and they always told her to be careful on the train. On some weekends, she stayed at our house and didn't do any cleaning or cooking, often taking the bus to White Plains instead. I knew not to visit her in her room when she returned those days, though I was tempted. My parents wouldn't mind if I was playing the word game with the TV on in the background.

Mary Jane checked her watch. "Five minutes left."

"How many do you have?"

"Not telling," she said, clutching her paper. "But a lot!"

I didn't like that Mary Jane ate by herself and used the phone only to call for cabs to the train station. When I asked, my mother said she and my dad loved Mary Jane and that she was welcome to do whatever made her comfortable in our home. We were George McGovern Democrats. My dad was the son of immigrants, self-made; my mom joined her store's union. Still, Mary Jane sat alone at the table and didn't use the phone. I wondered whether she was truly comfortable doing and not doing these things.

Mostly, I didn't like that Mary Jane, and Betty before her and Winnie and Annie Mae after her, served me, and I especially didn't like that the women were Black, aware even at nine of racial tension beyond our house. When I asked, my mother said that only Black women applied for the job. I was too young to understand that that, in and of itself, was a problem. But I felt something intrinsically wrong about it, and I felt bad for being in a house in which the women worked, though I loved them very much. I hadn't had the sensation before, something I can now define as guilt, and it simmered in me whenever I was around them, which was all the time.

When a new housekeeper was to begin working for us, Mom went to pick her up at Miss B's, the agency in Larchmont. The women sat in a row, lined up in chairs against the wall, overnight bags at their feet.

"Susie, come here," Miss B would say. "You're going to like this family."

Susie would shoot up in her coat and hat and my mother would say hello and take her in her Buick Skylark to our house, show her the spare room and the bathroom with the wallpaper that looked like gold vines were painted on it. It was just a powder room, so Susie would shower two flights up in the hall bathroom that my brother and I used, though she'd leave no trace, no towel or shampoo bottle or robe or pajamas. She'd wait until no one was home. Within minutes of stepping into our house, Susie would have put on a uniform and white shoes like a nurse and found the dishwasher, where she would wait for instructions.

I went through the letters in *transportation* again, starting with the T. Mary Jane had taught me the sequence trick. The results were not as exhilarating as they were when a word popped out unprovoked, but the strategy was thorough. Mary Jane was thorough.

When I got to the P, the plastic let out a clap and peeled off of the TV. It swung down and dangled from a corner, where Mary Jane had applied double tape. The man's face and hands and shirt flashed white, returning to their normal colors in a violent whoosh. I watched the tape on the corner begin to pull away from the set, dragged down by the weight of the plastic sheet, its crease now untethered and pulsing. Mary Jane lunged from the bed to grab it, but she, for all of her agility, did not get there in time. The sheet of plastic flew off the set, its two halves snapping together like a rat trap. It dove to the floor, hitting with slaps and buckles before landing. Mary Jane crouched to pick it up off the tile. The baby blue uniform rode up as she bent, and I saw a dark bruise on her thigh, inches wide and swollen. She pressed the plastic onto the set, but it sprung off into her stomach. She fumbled and caught it and tried again, flattening one palm on the back of the TV, pushing with the other in front. The plastic held for a flash before bursting off the glass onto her feet. She snatched it up and threw it into the basket on the bottom of the stand.

Mary Jane sat back down on the bed, and the mattress bounced beneath me, jerking my legs forward from the knees. She yanked the hem of her uniform over her thighs and picked up her paper and the TV guide.

"I think it's time," she said.

Mary Jane smoothed her hair into her neck and flipped up the ends. She let out a strong breath.

"Wait," I said, sliding off the bed.

She watched me go. At the door, I turned back to look at her. She flattened her palm over her dress, on top of the bruise.

I ran up the steps to my father's desk and found the gray tape that he used on the corners of our suitcases. In the bathroom, I grabbed the box of big Band-Aids from under the sink and then made my way back down to the spare room, one hand gripping the railing, the other cradling the supplies rolled up in my shirt.

Mary Jane was smirking at the TV when I walked in. The chartreuse man, now white, was in trouble again.

"He just can't help himself," Mary Jane said.

I reached into the folds of my shirt and retrieved the tape. She smiled sweetly at me and took it.

"You have to cut it with scissors," I said, still clutching the Band-Aids through the fabric.

Mary Jane got up to get a pair from her drawer, and I put the box on the bed. She turned from the bureau gripping the blades. "Let's make that silly man green again."

She bent to get the rainbow plastic from below the TV and saw the Band-Aids, halting for a split second, her face falling. Then she snatched the sheet from the basket and sat back down next to the box, tapping the mattress for me to come join her.

"I'll stretch out the tape, and you cut," she said, tilting her shoulder gently into mine.

I threaded my fingers into the holes and snipped, piece after piece, feeling her arm against mine until we were done.

FLUTTER KICKS

Through my bedroom curtains, I could see the flyboys leaving for the base, suited up in aviator sunglasses, cap and regulation aplomb. It was an invigorating way to wake up, a treat for both the voyeur and the patriot, two personas with which I had little rapport until then. Boys, as I knew them, didn't join the military and pilot jets. They forgot to get their hair cut, and they had little patience for authority. These guys were something else.

Fifteen thousand airmen worked at the base, which was just a few miles down the beach road. It seemed as if all of them were my neighbors in the garden apartments on Edgewater Gulf Drive, a busy place with orderly plantings and a swimming pool in the center yard.

I hadn't lived anywhere that had a pool, and I found the amenity to be something of a luxury. I dove in immediately after arriving from New York, even though it was only April and the local inhabitants were wearing snow gear. I kept my kickboard by the door.

Of all the television stations in the United States of America, the one in Biloxi, Mississippi, decided to hire me. Yes, they said, they wanted me to be their reporter, to cover fires and school board meetings, to climb onto fishing boats and interview shrimpers, all while looking authoritative, yet approachable, in blouses and bangs.

"C'mon down," they told me over the pay phone on Seventh Avenue, just outside the world renowned fashion showroom where

I worked in the press department but mostly folded sweaters.

"Really?" I yelled, buses and taxis and garment racks wheeling by.

"Yes, ma'am. We'll pay you thirteen grand—that's twenty up in Man-hattan."

Hmmm, I pretended to think, and accepted the offer.

In Mississippi, I spent long days digging for truth and justice. When I got home in the evenings and on weekends, I flutter-kicked laps and reclined on a lounge chair by the diving board. From my position, I could observe the flyboys' return march in the evenings as well as their leisure-time migratory patterns on Saturdays and Sundays. The men of the Air Force held their bodies firm when they walked, barely swinging arms or swiveling heads, stepping silently and beautifully and keeping their formation, even when turning off the walk to the parking lot. Serious pilots on terra firma, my neighbors at the Edgewater Terrace garden apartments engaged the mission at all times. Their life purpose pulsed through their corpuscles, rendering them potent and driven and thrilling, yes, to a Yankee girl on a chaise longue.

Of course, I did not speak with the airboys with whom I shared an address, not knowing, as a civilian, how to initiate that sort of contact or whether it was allowed, even, by the United States Armed Forces. So, I watched them from afar, hoping that one fine Officer might approach me, might say, "How are you today?" or "How's that backstroke coming?" or "Will you be my girl-friend, right now, please, and forever?" Needless to say, it was most enjoyable watching the flyboys from afar, as I had become smitten, no, exceedingly smitten with every single one of them at Edgewater Terrace in Biloxi, Mississippi. Every one, like that.

I sat at the pool one Saturday morning, reading a newspaper. A guy opened the gate and headed my way. He was shorter than the other residents and fluffy around the middle. His shoulders slumped forward, and his knees belled out. He did not have the airman silhouette, I saw instantly, unable to imagine his form in regular clothes, let alone the "service blues." The jacket sleeves would not hang creaselessly. The trousers would get trapped at the bend at the knee. As he approached, the tip of his sandal caught the cement, nearly catapulting him to the ground. Not a man for combat. In my two months at Edgewater Terrace, no Officer in the United States Air Force had said more than hello to me. Of the abundance of male talent in my midst, the cornucopia of strength and citizenship, of dedication and physical prowess, not one flyboy saw fit to pursue an exchange. The pool guy cleared his throat and wiped his hand on his shorts. He stomped his foot back into the sandal. I knew where this was going to go. And I knew that it would not go well. It was too late to fold up my towel and take off, and it was futile to avoid looking. The pool guy ratcheted the chaise next to mine to the desired angle, the conversation angle, and lowered his body down.

"Do you know how to play?" he asked, throwing open a back-gammon set.

I had won a high school tournament. "No idea."

"Here, let me teach you."

"That's okay."

"Oh c'mon, take a break from the paper." He set out the discs on the board. "You go first, clockwise."

If I left right then, he'd watch me walk home, and I did not want him knowing where I lived. I could have gotten into my car, but I didn't have the keys. I could have taken a walk to town, but I left my shoes inside, just a few steps away. Defenseless, I was, at the apartment pool.

"You from New York?" he asked, seeing that I was reading *The Times*.

"It's not a local paper."

He squinted. "I'm from New Jersey. Paramus."

"Heard of it." Home to my favorite store.

"Sure you don't want to play?"

Nodded no.

"Want to swim?"

Did he think that we were on a date? Did it appear to him that I wanted to share some kind of weekend summer activity with a presumptuous and klutzy stranger? Was he misreading the actual statements coming from my mouth, thinking that I said "Yes" instead of "No," or "Please talk more" or "I really like you, yes I do, come kiss me right now in between spins of the dice???"

He said that his name was Marty and that he was a Ground Radio Maintenance Technician at the base. He adjusted frequencies. After twenty-five minutes, I determined that Marty was not going to leave the pool area before I did and that my remaining in place would be construed as interest. It also occurred to me that a guy like Marty would find out where I lived, anyway. He would pester the manager in the rental office until she told him my apartment number, and then he would go there and wait. Until I walked out. Until I walked in. Until I tried to slip through the window behind the tree before dawn. So I packed up my pool bag and went home, wishing for him to stay behind. But my rejections left hope alive for Marty, like a palmetto bug after a half-baked whack. Had I been more definitive, had I said, "You know, Marty from Paramus, you are not for me. I want Southern, Marty, Southern, with blond-edged hair, Topsiders that don't trip on cement pool decks and a 'Sweetheart' attached to the ends of sentences. I want confident, Marty, with a smattering of well-placed freckles and a keen wit and a way with puppies,"—had I said all that, I wonder if he still would have followed me to my home at Edgewater Terrace and asked me to the movies.

"Let's go eat dinner, then," he said, when I turned him down.

"Bye bye," I said, closing the door.

The next weekend, I avoided the pool and bought a dress instead, high-necked like a Geisha's, with Japanese letters printed at whim. I will wear this on TV. It will make an enduring impression among viewers.

"I saw you on television, at the docks, with the shrimp boats," Marty said as I returned with groceries one evening soon after. He had been sitting on a bench near my apartment. "You were wearing a kimono."

He continued. "Hey, someone I know is having a party on Friday. Someone from the base, well, not really, but a civilian, someone who works near the base. Want to come?"

"Oh, thanks, but I can't."

"I've asked you out three times now, and you keep saying 'No.' Why don't you just say 'Yes' for once? It's not like you have another date or anything. You're not dating anyone else, are you?"

Else? I picked up my pace.

"So what's the problem?" Marty kept step. "All I've done is ask you out, nicely. Just agree already."

"My ice cream is melting," I said, pretending there was ice cream in my bag. "Bye, Marty."

"Yeah, you don't have ice cream." He smacked a tree with his hand.

I rolled apples and oranges into the fridge like balls from a pitching machine. I threw a sack of rice onto a shelf, bread into the freezer. I kicked the paper bags on the floor. Other girls get the right ones; I don't get the right ones.

Two days later, I found a note taped to my door. "My mother is coming to town on the 23rd. Can you have dinner with us? Marty."

Aaaaaaah.

"P.S. You have to eat, you know."

I do not.

Later, Marty called me on the phone.

"I can't," I said. "And please don't ask again."

"Ever again?

"Uh-huh."

"Well, I don't know if I can do that. I may just not do that."

A few weeks passed without communication, and I felt relieved that he had, in fact, given up. On the 23rd, the phone rang.

"Hello, is this Samantha? This is Marty's mother, Mrs. Gray."

"Hello?" she said again.

The voice was calm and caretaker-like, melodic, almost. The voice of a mammogram technician.

"Hello, are you there? Samantha?"

I fell onto my bed and covered my eyes.

"Hel-lo," Mrs. Gray sang.

No reasonable mother would do this. No mother, no matter how devoted, would call a stranger on the telephone for her grown-up Ground Radio Maintenance Technician son the second upon landing in Biloxi, Mississippi. I wondered if maybe she didn't want to be doing this exact thing. Maybe Marty was pressuring her, pummeling her with backgammon discs, holding her against her will in his efficiency kitchen at Edgewater Terrace.

"Hello," I said.

"There you are, dear. We were wondering if you'd like to come along for dinner this evening. Marty has told me so much about you."

Marty didn't know so much about me.

"Oh, gee," I said. "Thank you so much, but I can't."

"You can't?"

"No, I'm afraid I can't."

"What about tomorrow?"

"Oh tomorrow, I can't tomorrow either, but thank you."

"Not tomorrow either?"

"I'm afraid not, but thanks, really. Thanks so much."

"Oh."

"Okay, bye."

"Not tomorrow?"

"No, okay, bye."

Of course, I had no plans for that night, a Friday, or the Saturday twenty-four hours later, and I was now compelled to orchestrate some scheme to get myself out of the apartment under watch. I could stay home and fumble around with the lights out, maybe paper-clip some bath towels over the seams in the curtains, but Marty and his mom would spot the car. A-ha. A snob and a liar, they'd think.

I went to the movies. Just one, thank you. Small popcorn.

Afterward, I did not see or hear from Marty or his mother, Mrs. Gray. I was proud of myself for being clear and forthright. In graduate school, I retreated to the medical library for four consecutive days to avoid a boy from Iowa who wanted to marry me in a barn. A journalism student, I studied in the endocrinology stacks, believing it would be the last place the boy would look. I had matured, yes I had.

Two months later, Marty called again. "Sam, is that you?"

I thought to hang up.

"I'm in the hospital."

You can't hang up when someone is in the hospital.

"Why?" I asked.

"Oh good, it's you. I had a car accident."

"Are you hurt?"

"No, I'm not hurt."

"Then why are you in the hospital?"

"When you wouldn't have dinner with us, I drove my car into a wall, and they want to find out why I did that, so I'm in a hospital."

A psychiatric hospital, oh God.

"A psychiatric hospital."

"In New Jersey?"

Please say New Jersey.

"No, right here, in Biloxi."

"I'm sorry you are in the hospital."

"It's all right."

"Bye."

———————

My parents deployed my brother to Biloxi several weeks later, for routine reconnaissance. I would have to keep the Marty situation under wraps. If they found out, I'd be trailed by the sheriff for the rest of my southern stint and perhaps, my ensuing adulthood.

The day Dan arrived, I took him to cover a story at City Hall, and he walked around in the back of the shot. Later, we watched him on TV.

The next morning, a Saturday, the door knocked.

"Check first," I said, just as Dan turned the knob and swung open the door.

"Is Samantha Kent at home?" asked a woman in a white dress.

"That's me," I said, coming to the door. This wasn't any ordinary white dress, I saw up close, not a sheath from Calvin or tennis garb, even. This was a uniform, yes it was, and the woman in it, a nurse. A nurse with a uniform and a patient, in fact, standing next to her, an identification bracelet circling his wrist.

"Marty is out for the afternoon, and he wanted to come by and say hello."

Dan twisted his brows at Marty and then at me. I took charge of the door.

"Hi, Sam," Marty said.

"Okay, great," I said, turning to Dan. "We've got to run, don't we? Oh wow, we're so late. Okay, bye bye." I shut the door and leaned on it.

"That guy was a psych patient," my brother the surgical intern announced, peering through the edge of the curtain. "What are you doing having psych patients visit you?"

"You can't tell Mom and Dad. Really, you can't."

"Jesus, that was a psych nurse. It's against all protocol, showing up like that. The South, man, this place is crazy."

I slid down to the floor. "He kept asking me out and I kept saying no, so he drove his car into a median."

"What? On a highway?"

"I think." I pulled the curtain over my head and looked out of the corner of the window. "Oh God, he's just standing there."

"Of course he is. He's let out from a psych ward."

"Please don't tell Mom and Dad."

"Did he say he drove the car into a wall or are you imagining that?"

"He told me. On the phone from the hospital."

"Wow. That's incredible. And over you...unbelievable."

Dan found the name of the hospital in the local phonebook and called the medical director, requesting that Marty be prohibited from ever coming to my home again. He said he would report the nurse and the institution to the authorities if Marty returned.

"Man, Sammy, I'm telling Mom and Dad."

I felt responsible for Marty's accident though I knew, rationally, that another girl, at another time, could have driven him to drive into the wall and that I, for all my charms, was not that special. But, unarguably, it was this girl, me, at that moment on the clock, who prompted his wayward turn. To cope, I decided to view the incident as a case of probability. Leave the house three seconds later and avoid the fire. Run into your long-lost twin sister in a hot air balloon over Chile—it has to happen to someone. Still, I felt bad for Marty Gray from Paramus. His predicament would alter his life's course. Perhaps those in the position to help would now have their warning siren, and for that, I felt that I had made a valuable contribution. But the image of the aqua Camaro, on impact, remained in my mind, disrupting my composure like a pop-up clown at a carnival arcade.

I made a friend at the apartment complex, Marilyn, an Air Force rheumatologist from Roanoke, Virginia. She invited me along to a party not long after Marty's porch appearance. I wasn't sure that I wanted to go, let alone interact with a male person ever again, in Biloxi or beyond.

"Boys don't, as a rule, swerve their vehicles into highway blockades," Marilyn said, suggesting that I join her. "I know this. I'm a doctor."

"I think it was a median."

It was a casual get-together of officers and physicians from the base. On the way, Marilyn said that I might consider approaching a boy I liked, rather than waiting for an unsolicited one to choose me. It sounded like a sensible strategy, though I had been in the habit during my childhood, adolescence and early young adulthood of making no such overtures. But Marty's trajectory provided an impetus for change. We walked into the house to a lively crowd, energetic and conversant. Jackson Browne played in the background. This would be a safe place to practice the new selection technique, and I was happy that I didn't stay at home under the sofa.

"There's one, by the fireplace," Marilyn said. "Go, go."

The designated boy held his hands in his pockets, the way people do on verandas in Nantucket, or so I imagined. His skin, fair, and hair, blond, melded in lightness, radiating a golden glow to his adjacent space. He was a standing lamp. He was exquisite.

Other people surrounded him, I saw from across the room, as would be expected. He'd smell like soap-on-a-rope, nothing musky or floral, but the scent of the wind, zephyr soap. I breathed in deeply to see if I could detect the zephyr soap but inhaled the boy next to me, instead, catching a waft of something septic, formaldehyde, maybe. An Air Force pathologist, I'd later learn. I didn't think that I could walk across the room and introduce myself. It would feel too obvious, too aggressive, even. I'd turn an ankle or spill someone's drink.

"Now's the time," Marilyn whispered into my ear.

"He's too handsome. Maybe there's someone less beautiful, not the cutest one in the class. Third cutest."

"Just go, you can do it. No big deal."

I took a step toward the boy from Nantucket but twirled back around to where I began.

"It's too far. I can't cross an entire rug."

But I wanted to do something, something that I hadn't done before. I decided to stay put and transmit subtle karmic signals in the boy's direction. Before, I transmitted nothing, so this was progress. This was an attempt to disrupt the natural course of my psychosexual development until that point, a development characterized by superficial or humiliating or inept interactions with the opposite sex. I took notice of the boy, purely and gracefully. No stunts, no choreography. This male knew bone china from clay, an elegant backhand from a clobber. He would find me, or think that he had, a pearl among paste. I glanced at his eyes, his shoulder, the negative space that outlined his form.

"C'mon, Sam, you've got to do something."

"I am, I'm doing it right now. I'm transmitting. Watch."

"I don't see you doing anything."

"Look at my eyelids. And my chin. Lifting, now."

"Yeah, sort of. Do it some more."

I cocked my head slightly, letting my hair fall onto my cheek.

"Oh, that's good," Marilyn said.

"Is he looking?"

"Not yet."

I swiveled and brushed back a stray bang.

"Now?"

"He has shifted to his other leg and crossed his arms. Nice wrists. Leather watch band."

A flash of the eye. That would be my eye.

A turn of the lip. His.

"Movement, we have movement," said Marilyn. "I think you've done it. Wow."

I pretended not to notice when he excused himself from his conversation, brushed down his shirt, adjusted his wire-rims and navigated the room toward me. My follicles tightened. My throat narrowed.

"Hi," he said, offering a hand.

He was more than a standing lamp. He was a chandelier.

"Hi," I said, incredulous.

"I'm Peter."

"Samantha."

Flawless, he was. The manners. The understated flair. The ability to exchange appropriate dialogue. "How do you know Roger?"

"I know Marilyn, who knows Roger."

Let's get married. When I am ready, of course.

It took so little to get so far, staring into my future husband's eyes, bluish, with rims of amethyst. We would honeymoon in Montmartre and buy art from adorable men on the streets. He'd grill zucchini in khaki shorts. This is what it felt like. Finally, a boy I liked, liked me back. It was foreign and exhilarating. Why hadn't I done this sooner? Did I do this? I didn't know. But whatever had transpired, it was monumental. I had had instant crushes before; not one of them had crushed in return. This was a watershed.

We talked for nearly two hours before we discovered what each of us did for a living. Peter was an investigator for the Air Force's internal operations unit, the department that policed its own servicemen. If there was a problem, an insubordination or infraction of any kind, The Office of Special Investigations would conduct a probe. To hold such a position, he'd have to be precise and curious, like me. He'd have to be thorough and well-prepared, also like me. Compatibility zinged around our bodies, swooping and circling like figure eights.

"Can you tell me about a case," I asked, "or are they all privileged?"

"Some are, but I can describe certain ones. You can't put them on the news, though."

"Ooh, I can't promise that." Flirt, flirt.

Peter laughed and leaned his shoulder into mine. Zephyr soap, indeed.

"All right, there was a case recently about a guy, non-combat, who caused us some concern in his private life."

"What kind of concern?"

"Well, he was sort of obsessed with some girl, and certain things he did troubled us."

"I bet lots of boys at the base are obsessed with girls."

"Yes, and there are fifteen thousand of them, but not all of them do what this nut did."

"What did he do?"

"He drove his car into a wall when this girl wouldn't go out with him, if you can believe that. And no history of anything, so it's not as if he was a wacko to begin with. This sort of pushed him over the edge." Peter motioned his arm forward through the air to illustrate. "That edge is hard to see before people get to it."

A blast of cold swept up my lumbar region.

"What did you do with him?" My voice sounded like a machine.

We sent him to a psych hospital, I mouthed his words in my brain.

"Must have been some girl," he went on. "Wouldn't want to meet up with her."

Of course, you wouldn't. She would make you slam into a wall, too, or a stanchion or a guide rail. You, who would have zero control over your own responses to people who didn't do what you wanted them to, you would like never to come close to such a person, such a person who simply said no. No, thank you. You're not for me, despite your hounding, your stalking, your guilt-making, your transgressing. Was this girl whom you wouldn't want to meet have to have known about and therefore considered Marty's edge? Managed Marty's edge? Was it her responsibility to decipher his tenuous mental state while sitting on a chaise at the apartment pool? While feeling that she didn't want to eat dinner with him and his pushy mother? Was she supposed to be the Office of Investigations of Edgewater Gulf Drive? I expected more from Peter, beautiful luminescent Peter.

"Marty Gray," I said, replanting my feet. "I'm the girl."

"You're the girl?"

"I'm the girl," I said, queasy. "I'll just go now."

"No, wait." He ran a hand through his hair. "I didn't mean that, exactly."

"But sort of."

"Hey, you're a terrific girl. I can see why..."

I smiled. "Thanks."

"No, really, you are."

Doom descended. I found Marilyn and told her I'd wait for her in the car. I watched the mingling through the windows, reminded of the muted chatter that would float to my childhood bedroom from downstairs, where my parents were entertaining guests on the fancy plates. Peter didn't come out to find me. I thought he might have, even if only to peek.

THE DOODLES

J ack was a fine candidate for something called a Laser-Assisted Uvulopalatoplasty, a simple procedure in which the uvula is cauterized, making it smaller and less likely to obstruct the air passageway at the edge of the soft palate. An Ear Nose and Throat guy could do it in minutes. Maddie had been kept awake for months by the guttural explosions that burst from her husband's body each night and permeated the house, riding the waves up the attic ladder, down to the earthen crawl space and sideways to the couch down the hall. Her most effective strategy—swatting him in the chest or abdominal cavity—had proven useless. Before he became acclimated to the assault, Jack flipped to his stomach like a Pavlovian flounder or choked in enough oxygen to quiet down, at least temporarily. His failure to silence the cacophony had become uncharitable, if not torturous. The time had come, Maddie decided, eyes desiccated, constitution unraveled. He would have the insidious flap of tissue burnt out of his throat with a torch, under local anesthesia, of course. Though he had resisted for months, Jack finally agreed to see a doctor.

"A Laser-Assisted Uvulopalatoplasty?" Maddie asked at the consultation.

"Why, yes," the doctor said.

"Is it particularly fleshy? I mean, is it fleshier than most?"

"There's a lot of tissue there."

"Perfect. Can you take it out today?"

The doctor laughed. "First, we'll need to observe him overnight."

"Can we do that today? I'm so tired."

Of course, Jack hadn't completely agreed to have the procedure. He did say he'd spend a night at the sleep lab, though, for testing.

"They're probably going to hook you up to machines and stick things in your eyelids while you're in bed," Maddie said, on his way out at the end of the week.

"I can see that you're happy about this."

"Me? This is not about me. Now hurry. You don't want to be late. Go, go."

The night that Jack went to the lab, Maddie and the dogs went to sleep early and woke up late, uninterrupted. She had taken the day off from work in anticipation. That morning, they stayed in bed, ate toast and drank coffee.

By eleven o'clock, Jack arrived with the report, as well as circular impressions on his neck and forehead. "They woke me up every ten minutes. It was unbearable."

"Interesting, the unbearable part. What's on your neck?"

The dogs, doodles named Barney and Twyla, cocked their heads.

"That's nothing." He pulled up his T-shirt. Jack's trunk was speckled with aubergine dots, from the electrodes.

The doodles scooted back.

"So, what did they find out?"

"They said I snore."

"That's it?"

"I could've told them that," Barney said to Twyla.

"When's the procedure?" Maddie asked.

"I didn't say I'm going to have it."

Jack smelled septic, like gauze and cleaning fluid. The dogs sniffed his perimeter.

"Well, then you'll have to get the hose that shoots air into your trachea all night," Maddie said. "Maybe you want to get one of those instead."

"That thing would blow me across a room," said Twyla, the smaller doodle of the two.

Jack went into the bathroom to take a shower. The hot water made the dark circles on his skin even darker. He looked pretty funny, but he didn't laugh. Then, he got dressed and went to work, calling from the front door that he'd be home late.

After a few weeks, Maddie gave up on the Laser-Assisted Uvulopalatoplasty and slept every night down the hall on the couch. But then Jack announced that he was going to have the procedure after all.

"Hmmm," Barney said to Twyla. "Curious."

Maddie had adopted Barney first and Twyla, two years later. Each time, Jack had the same reaction: "I thought you weren't going to get the dog." Forget affection, the doodles wouldn't take a veal chop from Jack.

The singeing of the uvula took about fifteen minutes, after which Jack returned to work and continued his regular day. That evening, he sprayed emerald green liquid onto the affected area.

"Open up," said Maddie, wanting to see.

The throat cavity was outlined in black. A remnant of the uvula hung from the top, just a small droplet of skin, one-eighth its original magnitude.

"What a cute little uvula you have now," Maddie said, kissing Jack's cheek. "Did he say if it will grow back?"

"It can do that?"

Jack stuck out his tongue in the bathroom mirror and assessed the aftermath. "Hurts like hell," he gurgled, inserting the spray nozzle far into his mouth and aiming.

———————

Maddie and Jack, both thirty-two, had married three years earlier after a whirlwind courtship. Their physical attraction was undeniable, from the moment they met at a food truck in downtown Providence. They worked close by to one another and found ways to leave their offices and steal kisses on Westminster Street, leaning up against lampposts or tucked inside shop doorways. They said that they loved each other, over and over again.

After the procedure, Maddie rejoined Jack in bed for the entire night. At first, she woke within an hour, conditioned by many months of disruption. But after a couple of days, her body readjusted. She slept soundly and felt strangely alert in the morning.

Some days later, fourteen of Jack's office mates arrived for a dinner party. They could have gone to a restaurant, but Jack, in his position as leader of his department, offered up the house, a sweet Cape Cod on the East Side. The company sent caterers, who arrived early to prepare, carrying shiny tins of asparagus and potatoes and salmon, speckled in rosemary and dill. They laid out the food on the kitchen counters and whisked off the foil, releasing scents of pepper and lemon into the air. Barney and Twyla staked out positions underneath.

The people served themselves and sat down in the dining room at a long table. A co-worker sat on one side of Jack and his boss's wife on the other. Maddie positioned herself at the end, near the kitchen.

Jack took a bite of salad and winced, reaching for his throat. Then he pushed back his chair with his feet, his skin reddening.

"Oh god," said the co-worker next to him, turning in her seat. "Jack, are you okay?"

A man jumped up from the far end of the table. "I know the Heimlich," he called, grabbing Jack under the ribs.

Maddie ran to the kitchen to call 9-1-1.

The man pressed his fist into Jack's midsection, counted, and did it again. The other guests gathered around, palms over their mouths.

Jack threw his head left and right, fighting to peel the man's hands off of him. "Stop. Not choking, stop."

The man relaxed his hands but kept his arms hugged around Jack's torso. His chin rested on Jack's head, a totem pole.

Maddie ran back into the dining room. "Oh no, the uvula."

Jack nodded, sweating. "The tomato. Acidic."

"What's wrong with his uvula?" asked his boss, Larry. "And what's a uvula?"

It had been eleven days since the Laser-Assisted Uvulopalato-plasty, and while the doctor said that the sensitivity would have passed by then, it clearly hadn't. Jack must have had a delicate uvula.

"You mean that dangly thing?" asked Larry.

Larry's wife held her neck with two hands. "He had that cut out?"

Meanwhile, Jack and what was left of his incinerated uvula knocked around in the kitchen. He refilled his water glass and continued the dousing, pacing back and forth and making sounds, low-pitched groaning sounds.

Jim, an account executive, leaned into the doorway. "Can we look?"

"You don't want to look," said Jack, still gasping.

"Oh, come on," said Larry. "It's not like it's your penis."

"What!" yelled Jim, over the commotion. "What penis?!"

Barney and Twyla monitored the salmon in the oven and the hysteria in the dining room. In between the two rooms, there was an alcove, where they convened.

"Something's up with the blond lady," Barney told Twyla.

Twyla tilted her head. Her ear flopped into her eye.

"Something with Jack. Can you go under the table?"

"To do what?"

"C'mon, Twyls, think. Go under there and see if she's touching him. They do that. I saw it on TV."

"Wow. Okay."

"Report back in five."

Barney slept in the bed and knew what was going on in the bed, which was not much. During the previous six months, Jack and Maddie had sex infrequently, maybe three times at most. They hadn't been at odds, so Maddie attributed the lack of intimacy to her snoring-induced fatigue. She suggested that they rendezvous earlier in the evening, or on a weekend afternoon, but Jack's schedule didn't permit that sort of flexibility. He told Maddie not to worry, that they'd figure it out. After he said this, he'd usually put his arm around her, and she'd smile and fall asleep on his shoulder. At some point, he'd extricate himself, roll over the other way and begin snoring, waking Maddie up and sending her down the hall. In the eleven days since his uvula was burned from his throat and Maddie had joined him back in bed, they had sex just twice, triggering Barney's antenna. He would have sired six puppies by then.

Twyla's head emerged from under the table, the cloth a kerchief. "Her shoe is off, and her foot's on his ankle."

"I knew it. And in our house...despicable."

"What do we do?"

"We take care of it."

After dinner, the people went into the living room while Maddie helped the caterers in the kitchen. The blond co-worker plunked herself down in the chair next to the sofa, where Jack sat. Barney and Twyla stared at her and then at Jack. Barney squared himself in front of him, raised his lip and exposed his gum.

Twyla sidled up next to him. "You're not going to growl, are you?"

"I'd like to rip off his leg, if you want to know."

Twyla tried to mimic Barney.

"What are you doing with your mouth?" he asked, seeing her in the periphery.

"Not scary?"

"Scary like a chipmunk."

They staked out the room. Maddie entered with a tray of cookies that she had baked the evening before. The aroma sailed through the air currents over Barney's snout, and he trembled with restraint, focusing on the work at hand. Twyla jumped up and sat and twitched, unable to ignore the scent wafting over-head. Maddie placed the platter on the coffee table and sat down next to Jack, touching him on his knee. He laid his hand on hers without having to look. The blond woman stood and leaned over to pick up a cookie, her leg coming within centimeters of Jack's, her blouse falling open as she bent. Jack brushed back his hair, looked, and looked away.

"That's it," Barney said.

He shot up and approached the woman, a deep grumble intensifying as he closed in on her calf. Twyla followed behind him, looking left and right, unsure. The drone turned to a gnarl. Twyla pressed his haunch. The woman backed up, stepping her knees high, kicking. Losing a shoe. Jack lunged from the couch and reached for Barney, who met his movement with a throaty, wild warning. Jack recoiled, snapping his arm to his chest. "For Christ's sake, Maddie, what is wrong with him?"

Rumbling like an idling Corvette, Barney angled forward on his front legs, deltoids bulging. He lurched at the woman—for emphasis—before snatching her fallen cookie and sauntering out of the room.

Maddie looked for him down the hall and found him pacing by her desk near the front door. She sat on the floor, and he stepped into her lap, nuzzling his head on her belly. Twyla appeared and pushed herself under Maddie's arm.

"Lots of commotion, I know. They'll be gone soon."

———————

"I think it was a success," Maddie said later in the bedroom, stepping out of her skirt. "Apart from the tomato."

"God, the tomato."

"And our big scary guard dog. That was weird."

"Really, out of nowhere. He shouldn't be allowed to do that."

Maddie dabbed perfume on the side of her neck and got into bed, tapping the mattress. Hearing the invitation, Barney and Twyla trotted from across the floor and took a running leap.

"Not you two," she said, rubbing their ears.

"Just going downstairs a sec," Jack said from the door. "Think I left my glasses."

He filled a glass with water and sat on the living room chair, where the blond woman had been. He held the glass with two hands, his elbows resting on his knees. After a minute, he pushed himself straight, took a sip and headed for the stairs.

Barney had arrived quietly on the landing to observe and blocked Jack's ascent, standing watch, stiff, his tail raised over his back. Jack climbed the steps and hesitated at the top, saying nothing. Their eyes latched and narrowed. With a swoop, Jack stepped over Barney's trunk, swiping his ribs with the ball of his foot.

In the bedroom, Maddie sat up against the pillows in the quiet of the room and waited. Twyla lay curled into an oval next to her, eyes trained on the door.

"Find them?" Maddie asked when Jack entered.

"Hmm?"

"The glasses."

"Oh, yeah, no. I'll look tomorrow. It's late."

Moments later, Barney walked in, stepping gingerly. He saw that Twyla was on the bed and told her to stay put, making his way slowly across the room and onto the rug, forgoing his usual spot by Maddie's ankles.

Twyla walked to the edge, seeing his tentative gait. "Are you hurt?"

Barney shook his head. "I'm okay. You stay there, though."

She sat at the foot of the bed and stretched her legs forward. "You sure?"

"I just can't be near him."

Maddie turned toward Jack as he got under the blanket. She put her hand on his chest and kissed him.

He rolled over and settled into his pillow. "So tired. Long night."

Maddie and the doodles lay awake, restless. After a while, Twyla jumped off the bed and joined Barney on the rug, pressing her back into his. Maddie got up and dragged her blanket down the hall. And Jack slept, not a sound spilling from his roasted throat.

PHONE CALL

She was getting ready for bed when the phone rang, washing her face and putting on moisturizer, the yellow kind her mom swore by, from the bottle and not the tube. Jim, her roommate from Wisconsin, answered. He listened for a moment, handed it to her and watched, taking her afterward by the shoulder and sitting her down on the edge of her bed. He waited for her to say something.

A train derailed and careened off the tracks into the road beside it, where Samantha's parents sat in their Buick Electra Sedan. On their way home from a movie. Talking about Harrison Ford. Choosing the windows or the air conditioning, living not dying.

Jim walked her through the hall, calling to their other roommate to wake up. Adam, Adam. Get up. Now. Jim found Samantha's suitcases under the bed and put all of her clothing into them. Soon, she was in his car, in the back seat with Adam. She didn't know how Jim knew where to go, but somehow, they arrived at the Westchester Medical Center seven hours later, as the sun crept up over the Hudson.

A doctor led them to the room where her parents were. Jim and Adam waited outside the door, and Samantha went in. Her brother was on the way. The shock of the incident propelled her into some other plane of consciousness as they drove through the night from D.C., but she was utterly aware right then of the fact that she would be identifying two bodies and that the two bodies would be her parents. She hadn't seen a dead person until then. Maybe that was a good thing; she wouldn't be able to compare conditions. Were her mother and father more mangled than the previous dead person? Were they bluer or grayer or more bloated with fluids? More still? Less still? More dead? Less?

"I want to see it," she told the doctor, coming out of the room, "where it happened."

The doctor listened.

"Now. Before it's cleared away."

The doctor put his hand on Samantha's arm.

"Can you take me?" she asked her roommates.

Jim and Adam looked at the doctor for guidance. He blinked yes, reluctantly.

"We'll take you."

Samantha pulled her cardigan tight. "Do I just leave them?"

Jim and Adam drove her to the place where it happened and parked. It was mid-morning. Commuter trains had been rerouted, and the platform was still. A police car barricaded the scene; a couple of officers paced around it. Detectives would come look soon, and National Transportation and Safety Board officials would come, too. Samantha had interviewed one for a story about a tour bus crash on a Virginia interstate, the highest-ranking person that she had interviewed in her sprouting journalistic career. The woman's business card had a gold emblem on it. A drunk driver had hurled over the guard rail, sending the bus down the embankment. Jim, Adam and Samantha got out of the car and walked toward the track. Samantha grabbed the yellow police tape, pulled it over her head, and headed toward what remained of her parents' blue car. One of the policemen called out to her. His voice sounded as if it was in a cave, muffled and hollow. Samantha looked down at the grass underfoot, some blades pressed down flat, others gouged out from the earth. She stepped carefully, assessing their condition...pressed, gouged, pressed, gouged. The policeman took hold of her upper arm.

"I'm the daughter," she said. "I'm the daughter. The daughter."

He took a few more paces with her and slowed. Close enough. She stared at the debris.

"Was it thrown into the tree or just run over?"

The officer looked at his partner, who had come up alongside.

"Which?" Samantha asked.

The policeman who held her arm was fair and clean-shaven. He pinched the inside corner of his eyes with his free hand.

"It appears to me that…"

"Wait," Samantha said, turning to face him.

He stopped.

"Can you take off your hat? Are you allowed?"

He glanced at his partner, who nodded. Slowly, he peeled off the hat from front to back. Officer Lance T. Caldwell had reddish brown hair, straight and parted on the side. It was the kind of haircut that boys should have, nothing styled or fluffed.

"You have my mother's hair," Samantha said.

He squeezed his hat in both hands. Then he asked if there was anything that she needed, anything that the police force could do for her. He asked if she had relatives nearby and if Jim and Adam would be staying with her. He probably didn't think she'd ask again about how the car was struck.

"It appears that it could have been thrown," Officer Caldwell said, "but I am not sure."

Samantha thought for a minute.

"I suppose that's better. Better than the smashing. Right?"

Specific problems arise when you are orphaned at twenty-nine. Young child orphans go to live with relatives. Aunts and uncles swoop in and catch the little ones, making room at the kitchen table, buying new teddy bear sheets and blankets, packing another lunch for school. They worry about their tiny niece, and the pre-occupation with her loss and her emotional survival distracts them from their own. The other children watch out for her, including her in bike rides, remembering not to ask the questions that will make her feel sad or say the words "Mom" and "Dad." Then they say the words by accident and feel bad, crying to their own parents, who tell them that it is okay to make a mistake. They put their little hands around their cousin's shoulder before they would really know to do this, and the adults tilt their heads and scrunch their brows and well up with pride, feeling better about the horrible turn of events and lucky that their own children have been spared.

No one swoops in when you are twenty-nine and can make your own lunch.

"Better than the smashing, right?"

Officer Caldwell didn't think that it would have been better to be thrown than run over, or better to be run over than thrown.

"It is, yes," he told Samantha.

"Jim, Adam, it's better," she called to her roommates, turning to where they stood yards behind.

The sun hit her in the eyes, and she tried to shield them with her hands, making a tunnel of light. She stood squinting, having seen so much, seeing nothing.

HOLIDAY

Emily situated herself next to her sister in the back seat of the Toyota. "And we are going to Fredericksburg because...why?"

Her mother squinted into the rear view mirror. "It's historic and geologically significant."

"It's a strange place to go for a vacation."

"Oh, is it?"

Julia's children looked at each other that certain way, that Help Us, Please, Come Get Us way.

"And there are German beer halls in Fredericksburg, because of the settlers. With steins covering the walls."

Whispering in the back seat.

"I'd like to see the steins."

"You want to see cups on Spring Break?" Paige, the younger one, said.

"You know, you could have had a different kind of mother. Like Kyle Tooney's mother. Just imagine that sort of life experience."

Julia had booked an affordable bed and breakfast that looked pretty on the computer, a cottage on the banks of the Pedernales River. Rivers are good for get-aways. *We stayed on the banks of the Pedernales*, you could tell people afterwards. *Oooh. Sounds lovely.*

She and her middle schoolers drove the three hours from Dallas and spotted the cottage, turning into the dirt driveway in front.

"This doesn't look like the picture," Emily said.

"It's the place," Paige confirmed. "There's the bird bath. And the hearts on the edge of the shutters." Paige could see something once, and it would be impregnated in her visual memory. She did not need directions or a map. She was a human Global Positioning System, able to retrace her steps anywhere after just one trip, to the other side of town or across a small continent.

"Looks a little different in person."

Paige was not surprised. "It always does. Remember that place in Granbury?"

"C'mon, it's cute," Julia said. "We'll have to be careful walking by those metal scraps, though."

The girls giggled. "They're farm tools." They lived nearly their entire lives in Texas and knew of such things, unlike their mom, a transplant from the northeast. Always a saver, Julia was particularly frugal after the divorce. She worked for herself as an interior designer, sacrificing a more lucrative position at a firm in order to be available to the kids after school. They knew not to complain about downscale accommodations, nor would they think to, having observed their mother scramble to do everything on her own. Each night, they thanked her for dinner.

Julia parked the car on the grass. Down a little hill, they found the river. It was more of a stream, given the dry winter, but it was picturesque. The sun was strong, and the water flickered. On the far side, the land rose up in a well-worn slope, dotted with trees and rock and grass. There was nothing pristine or precious about the Pedernales; it was rugged, handsome. A fat Labrador ran out of one of the cottages, falling down on her back for a rub. A woman followed her out.

"You must be the Thomases," she said, holding out a rough hand. "How about that Rosie, girls? You got a friend for life in that one."

Emily and Paige stood up to greet the woman, Dottie. "Yes, ma'am," they said in unison.

Julia loved the ma'am.

"Y'all are in the Bluebonnet Cottage, my favorite."

"Excellent, the state flower," Julia said. "Kids, the state flower."

"Okay, Mom."

Dottie handed Julia the key. "Breakfast's at seven over there in the purple house. Come hungry."

There wasn't much else to know, and Dottie disappeared

as quickly as she had arrived. Julia and the girls brought their bags inside before heading to town for a walk. The screen door slammed the way a screen door does. The sound of the country, of lemonade. Of the radio in sticky air.

A few miles from Dottie's, they hit a wide boulevard, lined on both sides with painted white storefronts, benches and oil lamps. There was a park halfway down the street, and an old brick City Hall. Ducks walked around the cannon out front; one sat in the hole. Brave duck.

They went in and out of every single shop in Fredericksburg, smelled all of the candles, tried on every handmade necklace. They watched a potter pot, listened to a strummer strum, and ate an early dinner. In a German beer garden, yes, with steins on the wall and schnitzel on the menu.

Julia ordered a beer, a strawberry beer, because that is what you do in a German beer garden when you are on vacation in Fredericksburg, Texas.

"Are you going to drink that?" Paige asked. "It looks disgusting."

"I am, and here I go."

The girls grimaced.

"Tastes like watermelon," Julia said, sipping. "Do you know anyone who drinks beer?"

Paige slapped her forehead. "Mom, I'm twelve."

"Emily?"

"I know of some kids."

Paige whipped around. "You do? That kid Brady?"

"Well," Julia said, "*you* won't ever drink beer, underage, or any alcohol, or smoke or do drugs or get pregnant. You know I'd kill you if you did."

"Mom, we're not doing any of that, don't worry."

"Stay a virgin, that's all I have to say."

"Oh my god." The girls laughed, kind of, and looked around to see if anyone heard. An infant screamed at the next table.

"Need I say more?"

The kids' father had taken them on fancy vacations with his

new wife, whom he married two years after the divorce. They had seen Mickey Mouse and ordered croque monsieur from room service and come home with suntans. Two weeks before the Fredericksburg trip, the new wife sued Julia for slander, not liking something she had said. Though even the new wife's lawyer said the suit was really just a form of harassment, Julia was forced to hire an attorney to defend her. He cost four trips to Fredericksburg.

Julia hoped that the girls' excursions with her would be more meaningful than the frivolous ones they took with their father and just as, if not more, fun. To her, the time away from home really felt like a vacation. Without the hour-to-hour responsibilities of the kids' schedules, her work and household tasks, Fredericksburg could have been Paris. She didn't tell the kids about the lawsuit, the sixth one her ex-husband hurled at her, and she decided not to think about it during the three days they were in Dottie's backyard.

Hill Country sky was glorious at five in the afternoon. You needed sunglasses until nearly seven. Julia and the girls left the Schulz Garten Restaurant, their bellies full of schnitzel and sauerbraten, and stumbled upon a glass blowing studio around the corner. A man melted a rod into a schooner with drippy sails and gave it to them, still warm.

Back at the Bluebonnet Cottage, they sat on a garden swing near the pile of farm equipment and took photographs of each other while the sun went down. Later, before going to sleep, they lined up in the fold-out couch and watched a videotape, a romantic comedy from the 1980s. They could hear the cars drive by on the road outside the window. It was an odd vacation, the girls were right about that. Better, though, than the time when they drove seventy miles to see the dinosaur fossils, only to find them filled with so much rainwater that they were obstructed from view.

Julia got up and made sure both locks on the door were secure. When the girls closed their eyes, they looked exactly the same from the cheekbones up. When they opened them, they hardly looked related. There is a lot in the eye.

———————

The Thomases were the only patrons at the bed and breakfast that week, despite its reputation for being the busiest stretch of the season.

"It could be just us for breakfast," Julia whispered on the steps outside the purple house. "Just forewarning."

"That could be weird," Paige said.

"You want to get some asthma?"

"I can't just *get* asthma, Mom."

"You did it for the policeman that time, when I was going too fast in the school zone."

"I can't believe you two," Emily said. "Shhh, she's coming."

Dottie pulled open the door with a whoosh. "Good mornin', y'all. Hungry?" Bacon air smacked the Thomases on their heads.

Stomachs full, they headed for the main attraction, The Enchanted Rock.

Julia turned the ignition. "That wasn't too awkward, was it?"

"Her nine-year-old granddaughter served us and then went and played with her toys next to our table," Emily said. "How is that not awkward?"

"She had that same jumping thing that we had, that you put on your ankle," Paige said. "I loved that."

"Me, too, and those biscuits were incredible," Emily said.

Julia slowed at an intersection. "You didn't eat that congealed liquid stuff, did you?"

"It's called gravy, and yes, we ate it. You have to. It goes with the biscuits."

"It's a coronary, that gravy. Don't eat it again."

In the distance, a gargantuan hump of pink stone rose up from the brush.

"And gravy is for meat, not for baked goods. The Texans, man, they maraud the language."

The rock was shaped like a dome, smoothed out and symmetrical, an inverted bowl. It was a monadnock, the part of a huge igneous batholith that is visible above ground. Archeologists believed that human beings lived on or near the rock eleven thousand years earlier, and that it was made from material that was six million years old.

"Kids, look out the window!"

"Is that it? It's pink!"

"Who is having a weird Spring Break now? Not us, that's who."

They drove a few more miles and reached the base of the formation, where they parked and got out.

"Just lean up against the side of the car for a sec," Julia said. "You have to see it like this, on an angle. Look up."

The girls tilted back on the Toyota. It was a cloudless day; the mound's edge cut the sky into a turquoise crescent.

"Imagine that you are Tonkawa Indians staring up at the magical rock," Julia said. "Tonkawa Indians with a mid-sized sports utility vehicle."

Family court prevented Julia from returning to the northeast with her girls, and making a life for herself in a place where she didn't want to be proved difficult. But staring into the sky, a tiny speck of an organism, Julia wondered if her exile away from everyone and everything she knew could in fact be something that she needed, maybe something that everybody needed. She had no valid reason to think this, but the majesty of the land formation before her transformed her outlook, infusing it with uncharacteristic magnanimity and hope.

"How long do we have to stay like this," Emily asked. "My neck hurts."

"We're done. Let's go climb the thing, shall we?"

The rock had a subtle grade, not something for carabiners or funny shoes. Julia and the girls navigated the crevasses and rested on the stacks of stones that dotted the way. Brush and bramble stuck out through the cracks, finding sustenance somewhere beneath the polished surface. Nothing quite made logical sense about The Enchanted Rock. About three-quarters of the way to the top, the terrain steepened, and the number of climbers trailed off. Not one to take physical risks, Julia decided they should forego the Tonkawas' fire spot. It was a ridiculous concept, anyway, that they sat around and lit flames at the top. Fire can't come out of a monadnock.

The half-moon crept over the top of the dome, moving fast. Though solid and stiff, the earth did seem busy on The Enchanted Rock.

"Mom, your phone."

"It's okay, I can get it later."

They took photos of the view, fifteen hundred feet above sea level. The ringing persisted.

"Maybe it's important," Emily said.

"You can't just answer a phone on The Enchanted Rock. It's not what you should be doing at a place like this."

"At least look at the number," Paige said.

Julia wasn't interested. "Can you see any cities from up here? Or is it all wilderness?"

The person hung up and called again. "All right, that's it," Paige said, unzipping the pocket on her mother's backpack. "It says Attorney's Office."

Julia took the phone, losing her balance. The mere sight of the word, attorney, triggered palpitations and chills. Emily grabbed her arm. "Who's that?"

"It's nothing." Julia sat on a boulder.

"Are you going to answer it?" Paige asked. "You're sweating."

Though Julia had shielded the girls from a lot of the divorce litigation, she kept them apprised of key issues that would affect them, as they were of the age to form their own opinions.

"This has nothing to do with your father and me, so don't worry. It's some other silliness. Truly."

Despite her physical response to the call, an involuntary panic that she anticipated would remain for all of her days, Julia figured there was news about the new wife's lawsuit, and she expected it to be good. She'd listen to the message later.

They got up from the rocks on which they were sitting and traversed the hill sideways, encountering fellow hikers who advised on routes to take around the girth of the mound. Some of them, in fact, had the carabiners and funny shoes.

"Did you go up to the fire spot?" Julia asked one.

"You can cook out here?"

"No, the ancient…"

The man called to a woman yards away. "Suze, she says you can grill out here. Shoulda brought burgers."

Julia motioned to the girls to keep walking. They climbed

around the rock for an hour or so more and then headed down. At the bottom, Julia pulled out the phone and listened to the first message.

"Call me back when you can," Tim, her attorney, said. "It's important. Nothing to worry about, but call me back. Or Lindsey."

She listened to the second.

"Hey, Julia. Tim here. So, we've got a situation. Hate to leave a message, but we need to get on it quickly. Seems they're now saying you're, uh, unfit. Of course that's not the case, you're an incredible mother, and we can handle it, but we've got to get your divorce lawyer involved. I'm a civil attorney as you know....."

The rest of his words spun into an echoing vortex. Julia bent over and threw up, Dottie's eggs and biscuits catapulting through her innards and slapping onto the dirt. The girls ran toward her and held her hair back and took out tissues as she shook, in spasms, and wretched again. She knew what unfit meant. She knew the Texas courts. She saw it all, the terror that came to her at night, the ripping away of little bodies, the screams.

She wiped her face and held onto Emily and Paige, wanting to tell them, wanting them to know. She ran through the checklist... would it hurt them, would it make them stronger, would it make them safer, wiser, better? Is it time?

"You okay, Mom?"

She held their faces in her hands. Eyes open, they looked the same, the first time. They looked afraid. "I'm okay."

"You sure? You're still shaking."

"It must have been the gravy."

Paige squinted in the Fredericksburg sun. "You had the eggs and a biscuit and no gravy. And a bite of bacon."

"I had a little gravy, I think. But who knows. Just hit me funny."

Julia pulled them closer and tighter, gazing toward the mound of rock rising behind them. It swept up in a swollen fecund curve, an impregnated belly of stone. The fertility of the scene was not lost on her, that such a threat to her babies would be lodged at this singular mystical place, this holy dome of earth that had made its way into the light, inch by inch. It was a heinous act at such a glorious spot, a wondrous mingling of science and spirit. Of Tonkawa Indians and sprouting vines and little girls. Mothers and beer steins. Adventures and hopes. The three of them stood, holding on, the spectacular bend of granite stretching out across Texas and Louisiana and Georgia, right smack into the Atlantic, or so it seemed.

ABOUT THE AUTHOR

Pamela Gwyn Kripke is the author of the novel, *At the Seams*, and the memoir, *Girl Without a Zip Code*. She has written features, essays and news stories for publications including *The New York Times, The Chicago Tribune, The Chicago Sun-Times, The Dallas Morning News, The Huffington Post, Slate, Salon, New York Magazine, Parenting, Redbook, Elle, D Magazine* and *Creators Syndicate*. Her short fiction has been published in *Folio, The Concrete Desert Review, The Barcelona Review, Brilliant Flash Fiction, Book of Matches, The MacGuffin, Meet Me At 19th, The Woven Tale Press, Underwired, Doubleback Review* and *Round Table Literary Journal*. She holds degrees from Brown University and Northwestern University's Medill School of Journalism and has taught at Columbia College and DePaul University. She lives near Philadelphia and has two daughters.

Made in the USA
Las Vegas, NV
03 April 2024

88200438R00090